BRIDE IN TROUBLE

by

SERENITY WOODS

DEDICATION

To Tony & Chris, my Kiwi boys.

CONTENTS

Chapter One

Slowly, she opened her eyes.

She lay in a narrow bed with crisp white sheets tucked around her. To her left, the sunlight streamed through large windows. The sky outside held a faint blush—early morning then, maybe six or seven a.m.

Dark-blue curtains framed the windows and complemented the blue walls and light-gray floor. The room looked clean but impersonal. A photo of a tree in a field that could have been anywhere decorated the wall opposite.

Beneath the window, a man sat in a chair, reading a book. He had short brown hair and a handsome, kind face, and he wore jeans and a white tee. He was maybe late twenties or early thirties. He'd rested one ankle on the opposite knee, and he was leaning his head on a hand, engrossed in whatever he was reading. He looked as if he'd been there a while.

Without moving her head, she moved her gaze around. Her right arm rested on the sheet, a piece of sticking plaster holding the needle inserted into the back of her hand. From it, a drip led to a bag of fluid hanging from a metal frame.

She was in hospital.

Glancing down, she looked at the rest of her body. Her legs were visible as mounds beneath the bedclothes, and when she wiggled her toes, both sides moved. She didn't feel as if she'd had an operation anywhere, but she ached all over, and she could see several grazes on her arms. When she tried to roll her head on the pillow, she received a sharp stabbing pain to the base of her skull.

Lifting a hand, she brought it up to her face. Her fingers found a bandage that went all the way around her head as if she were a mummy. She followed it and found—just behind her right ear—a large pad that obviously covered a serious wound, judging by how tender it felt and how much her head was now throbbing.

The man sitting opposite her glanced up at that moment. He stared at her for a second, then hurriedly got to his feet and came over.

"Hey." He reached out and took the hand she was touching to the bandage. "You're awake."

She moistened her lips and swallowed. "Could I have a drink?" she whispered.

"Of course." He turned and poured water into a cup from a jug on the table beside them, then passed it to her, supporting her hand as she took a few sips from the straw. When she nodded, he placed it back on the table. "How are you feeling?"

"Hazy."

"That's just the morphine." He rubbed her arm affectionately. "You were in a lot of pain."

She touched the bandage again. "My head hurts."

"Well, that's to be expected."

"Why? What happened to me?"

His green eyes surveyed her face for a moment. "What do you remember?"

She looked away, trying to recall the event, but it was like searching in gray fog. She had vague images of people standing around the bed, asking questions. She remembered crying because she didn't know the answers, as if she'd been taking an exam for which she hadn't revised. But she didn't remember arriving at the hospital, or what had happened before that.

"You had an accident," the man said gently. "You were out running, and a car came out of a side road and knocked you down. You hit your head on the ground and did quite a bit of damage."

That explained the bandages and the horrid headache.

He pursed his lips. "Do you remember your name?"

She blinked at the strange question. "Of course. I'm Phoebe Goldsmith."

He smiled. "That's a good start. Do you know where you are?"

"In hospital."

"Which town?"

"Whangarei?" It was a guess—it was the nearest hospital to where she lived in Kerikeri, the pretty town in the Bay of Islands, New Zealand.

"Yes, that's right." He tipped his head to the side. "Do you know who I am?"

She went to say no, then frowned. He was familiar… Her brain seemed to be working slower than normal, like a computer with a crap processor that took twenty minutes to start up in the morning.

Rebooting… rebooting…

Then realization dawned, and her frown deepened. "Dominic?"

He nodded, and his face lit with relief. He'd been afraid she wouldn't remember her own brother.

"You're going gray," she said with amusement, spotting the color at his temples. "And you look… different." She was being polite; she meant that he looked older. Not bad older, just… older. In her memory, he had a lean, almost slender, physique, with hollows beneath his cheekbones and a rangy frame. Now, his arm muscles stretched the sleeves of his tee, his shoulders and neck muscles were solid, and he just looked more… mature. Something didn't feel right. Her frown returned. "What's going on?"

He opened his mouth to reply, but at that moment the door opened. Phoebe looked over to see an older woman entering the room. She was tall and slim, and her face was familiar, although, like her son, she looked older, with fine lines around her eyes and mouth. The long blonde hair that Phoebe remembered was cut in a bob.

"Mum!" Phoebe felt a rush of relief at the sight of her mother.

"Sweetheart." Noelle Goldsmith put down the bags she was carrying on a chair, then strode over to stand the other side of the bed. "Oh, you're awake. That's wonderful. How are you feeling?" She leaned forward to place a heartfelt kiss on Phoebe's cheek.

"My head hurts."

"I'm sure it does, sweetie, it's had a terrible bang."

"Almost shook your brain out of your ears," Dominic said. His jollity was forced; he and their mother were looking at each other, she raising her eyebrows, he giving a small shake of his head, having a silent conversation.

Phoebe looked from one to the other, her heart hammering on her ribs. "How long have I been in a coma?"

"You haven't, darling," Noelle said. "Not really. You lost consciousness for about an hour. You've been in and out of it because of the morphine, that's all, sleeping mostly."

"For how long?" Phoebe said, bewildered.

"Only since Thursday," Dominic said. "Today's Saturday."

"What's the date?"

"The fourth of February."

Phoebe swallowed hard. "The year, Dominic. What year is it?"

Both he and their mother went still. "What year do you think it is?" he asked.

"I… I'm not sure…" She watched them exchange a worried glance.

"Sweetheart, it's 2018," Noelle said, resting a hand on hers. "Don't you remember?"

Phoebe's heart was racing, and it was making her head pound. This didn't make any sense.

"Where's Dad?" she asked. She needed her father. Sound, solid, and sensible, he had a way of making everything seem as if it was going to be all right.

Dominic and Noelle exchanged a long glance. "I'll get the nurse," Dominic said, and he strode across to the door and left the room.

Noelle picked up her hand and cradled it in her own. "Darling, Dad died just over a year ago."

Phoebe stared at her in horror. "What?"

"It's the accident, it's obviously jostled your memories around a little. I'm sure everything will get back in the right order when the swelling goes down, please don't worry."

How could she not worry?

"Daddy," she whispered, and her eyes filled with tears. Her head pounded, and she lifted a hand to it with a moan, closing her eyes, afraid they were going to pop out of her head. It felt as if someone had inserted a knife between her skull and the top of her spine, and was twisting it slowly.

Her mother's hand left hers, she heard a click, and then she felt a rush of something enter her bloodstream. Instantly, the knife in her skull withdrew, and the pain eased to a dull throb. Through half-opened eyes, she watched the room begin to fade away.

"It's all right, Rafe's on his way," Noelle said, taking her hand again. "That'll make you feel better."

Phoebe opened her mouth to ask who Rafe was, but couldn't get her lips to form the words. Sleep overcame her, and she sank slowly into oblivion.

*

The next time she woke, the sun was high in the sky and the room was hot. Her head hurt, but it wasn't throbbing as badly as last time. She shifted on the bed, and the nurse standing beside her smiled.

"Hello, Phoebe! Good to see you awake again. How are you feeling?"

"Better."

"Good. Want to sit up?"

"Oh, please."

The nurse lifted the back of the bed. "I'm going to check your blood pressure and a few other things, okay?"

"Okay." Phoebe watched her bustling around. "Where are my mother and brother?"

"Oh, they'll be in soon. You have quite a contingent here to see you. They were all talking too loudly, so I sent them down to the TV room. I'll let them in when you're ready."

Phoebe nodded, lifting a hand to touch her head. "Do I look awful?"

The nurse smiled. "A little tired, but not too bad. Maybe you'd like a quick bath before seeing everyone?"

"I'd love that." She gestured at the drip in her hand. "Can you take this out? It's uncomfortable."

"It's how we've been administering the morphine," the nurse said. "But I can take it out and give you pills if you need them now you're up and about." She came over, peeled off the sticking plaster, and withdrew the needle. "There." She pushed the tray of equipment away. "You're doing very well, dear. It won't be long and you'll be feeling more like your old self, I'm sure."

"What about my memory?" Phoebe said softly.

The nurse stopped and studied her for a moment. "Do you still not remember the accident?"

"It's much worse than that, I'm afraid. I appear to have lost quite a few years."

"Hmm." The nurse pursed her lips. "The doctor will be around this afternoon, and he'll be able to tell you more about that."

"Will I get my memory back?"

"It depends." She patted Phoebe's hand. "Don't worry about it right now. Let's get you in the bath and cleaned up, and then you can see your family."

"Can you get my mum to help me?"

"Of course." The nurse started the bath running, then left the room.

Phoebe lay there and looked out of the window until her mother arrived.

"Sweetheart, oh you look better," Noelle said, walking up to the bed.

"I feel better. Still tired, though. The nurse said I could have a bath."

"That sounds like a great idea. I'll check the water."

When it was ready, Noelle and the nurse supported Phoebe while she got to her feet, making sure she didn't feel too woozy, and then they led her into the bathroom.

"No getting your dressing wet," the nurse cautioned. "I'll be outside if you need me."

Noelle helped her daughter remove her hospital gown, and then made sure she got into the water safely. "I'll be outside," she said.

"No, stay, please." Phoebe gestured to the toilet next to the bath, and Noelle smiled and sat on the seat.

Phoebe put her arms around her knees, just enjoying the heat of the water, letting it soak into her limbs. She had scratches all over her arms and legs, and a big graze on her knee that stung, but it was nice to feel clean.

"Let me scrub your back," Noelle said. She knelt beside the bath, put a little soap on the sponge, and rubbed it slowly across her daughter's skin.

Phoebe leaned her cheek on her knees. "Is Dad really gone?"

Noelle paused for a moment, then continued washing. "I'm sorry, love, but yes. Just over a year now."

"How did he die?"

"He had a heart attack." Noelle's hand stopped for a moment. She squeezed the sponge tightly in her fingers. Then she carried on washing Phoebe's back.

"It's so odd," Phoebe whispered, tears stinging her eyes. She couldn't bear to think about her father not being around, not yet. She'd have to process that later.

Noelle reached out and tucked a strand of hair behind her daughter's ear. "You really don't remember?"

"I've been trying to think what the last thing is I can remember. It's all a bit muddled. I think… it's the day I left to go to Auckland University."

Noelle stared at her. "You don't remember anything after that?"

"No. Nothing."

Noelle had gone white. "You were only eighteen."

"And now I'm…" Phoebe calculated. Her birthday was in September, and Dominic had said it was February. "Twenty-six?"

Noelle nodded.

"Eight years. I've lost eight years." She felt a swell of panic, and immediately her head started to thump.

"Easy." Noelle brushed the sponge down her arm. "I've been doing some reading about amnesia, and it's quite possible your memory will come back in time."

"But what if it doesn't? What if those eight years have been knocked out of my brain?" Phoebe couldn't comprehend what that would mean going forward. How could she get on with her life when she couldn't remember if she had a job, or what all her friends and family were doing? She had no idea what movies were popular, what music. There might have been a world war for all she knew. Maybe there had been a natural disaster that had swept away half the country.

"The main thing is that you're here, and you're awake, and we'll deal with anything else that happens one step at a time," Noelle said.

Phoebe swallowed hard. "Okay."

"How are you feeling? Are you up to seeing some people? Everyone's desperate to see you with their own eyes to make sure you're okay."

"Who's here?"

"All the family," Noelle said, "except Dominic—he's had to go to work."

"Elliot," Phoebe said, naming her other brother.

"Yes. And both your sisters."

"Roberta," Phoebe said. "And Bianca." She smiled. Bianca was her identical twin. They'd always been close. She would be out of her mind with worry.

"They can't wait to see you," Noelle said.

Phoebe nodded. "I'd like to see them." She frowned then, remembering her mother's words just as she'd fallen asleep that morning. "Earlier, you said 'Rafe's on his way,' and that he would make me feel better. Who's he?"

Noelle squeezed out the sponge and put it by the taps, then turned to get a towel. "Why don't we wait and see if you recognize him? If anyone's going to jog your memory, it's going to be him. Now come on. Let's get you out, and then I'll brush and braid your hair for you."

Five minutes later, she was out, dried, and wearing comfortable track pants and a T-shirt that had the slogan *In Training for the Zombie Apocalypse* that Noelle told her was one of her favorites.

"I don't get it," she said, looking upside down at the slogan.

"You like to run." Noelle steered her over to the mirror.

Dominic had told her she was running when the car knocked her down. "Do I?" The statement baffled her. She'd played some tennis at high school, and netball, and she hadn't been bad at the high jump, but she wouldn't have called herself an athlete. The only time she'd have been interested in running anywhere was to get to a sale at the local chocolate shop. "I don't…" The rest of the sentence faded on her lips as she looked into the mirror.

She saw a pale face with a graze on her cheek, big green eyes with dark shadows beneath them, and a head swathed in bandages. She looked the same as she remembered, almost.

"I've lost an awful lot of weight," she said.

"It's all the training." Noelle emptied the bath.

"For what?"

"You're doing a triathlon next month. Well, you were." Noelle gave her a hesitant smile. Careful to avoid the wound, she began to brush Phoebe's hair.

"Jesus. Seriously?"

"You've changed a lot since you were eighteen, sweetheart. But don't stress. We'll bring you up to speed later." She braided Phoebe's hair over her shoulder and tied it with a band. "Let's get you back in bed, and then we'll bring the others in."

Phoebe let her mother lead her back to the bed, and she climbed on top of the covers, exhausted already from the exertion of taking a bath.

"Not long," the nurse stated when Noelle said she was getting the rest of the family. "We don't want to tire her out." She pulled the movable table around, placing it across the bed. It bore a tray with several dishes. "Lunch," she said. "Eat up—you need to get your strength back."

Phoebe smiled, but was too nervous to eat as she waited for the others to arrive. She sipped the orange juice, her heart thumping as she heard voices coming along the corridor. Would they have changed much? What if she didn't recognize them?

But she needn't have worried. As soon as Elliot walked in, she knew it was him. Like Dominic, he looked a little older, but his grin hadn't changed a bit.

"Sis," he said, and came over to give her a hug. "God, it's good to see you awake."

"Can't get rid of me that easily." She hung onto him for a moment, then let him go. Beside him stood a young woman, her dark hair pulled back in a ponytail, and another young woman who looked just like herself, with blonde hair tumbling around her shoulders. Both of them were crying, and her own eyes welled up as they came forward to hug her.

"Jesus, don't fucking do that to us again," Roberta whispered furiously. "You scared the shit out of me."

Phoebe laughed, despite the tears leaking from her eyes. "I'll do my best not to."

"I knew something was wrong," Bianca said, coming forward to hug her. "I could feel it. Is that stupid? I know it's stupid. But when Mum called, I knew what she was going to say before I picked up the phone."

"Born together, friends forever," Phoebe said. "That hasn't changed."

Bianca sniffed and exchanged a glance with the others. Phoebe frowned, but before she could query it, her mother was pushing them away and saying, "Come on, give her some space. She needs to eat her lunch."

"I definitely need to put on some weight." Phoebe wiped her face and peered beneath the cover over one of the plates. "I never thought I'd be able to call myself skinny." She picked up a piece of cheese, placed it on a cracker, and took a bite. Then, conscious that they'd fallen silent, she looked up to discover them all exchanging glances again.

"Mum said you've got amnesia," Bianca said. "Is that true?"

Phoebe swallowed the mouthful and nodded slowly. Cold filtered through her, and she looked at the cracker for a moment. She wasn't sure if she was ready to talk about it yet.

"We'll wait until the doctor's been and examined her before we get too worried," Noelle said. "He'll know more about it all."

Phoebe had another bite of the cracker and cheese as Elliot changed the subject, talking about how terrible the coffee was from the machine, and Roberta gave him a smart comment that made him laugh. In a way, none of them seemed to have changed from the way they were when they were all kids at home. But obviously they *had* changed. They'd grown up, and they would all have left home. Elliot was… what? Twenty-nine now, and Dominic must be thirty-two. Christ. Were any of them married? Did they have kids? Her head ached when she tried to think about it too much.

A movement at the door caught her eye, and she glanced over. A doctor stood there, dressed in a white coat, holding a clipboard, talking to a man. The man was listening to him, but he was looking at Phoebe.

For a moment, she felt as if someone had sucked all the air out of the room. The guy was tall, maybe six-one or two, with short dark-brown hair that stuck up as if he'd been running his hands through it all morning. He wore jeans and a gray hoodie, and well-worn black Converse shoes with white trim. He was incredibly good looking, and her first thought was that maybe a movie star was doing some kind of charity visit to the hospital or something. But the way he was looking at her told her he wasn't here by chance. He knew her.

He held her gaze for a long moment, and she swallowed the second mouthful of cracker with difficulty. Then he looked back at the doctor, nodded, and said something else before coming into the room.

"The doc will be back in a minute," he announced as he approached the bed. He had a deep, rich voice, and the hairs rose on the back of her neck.

"Thanks," her mother replied, looking at Phoebe. They were all looking at her. They were waiting for her reaction.

"Hey," the guy said. Up close, she could see that his eyes were a bright blue. He was gorgeous.

He was also a complete stranger.

"I'm sorry," she said softly, heart racing. "I don't know who you are."

Roberta turned away, Elliot looked at the floor, and Bianca pressed her fingers to her mouth.

The guy glanced at Noelle, then slid his hands into the pockets of his jeans. "I'm Rafe Masters," he told her. "I'm the guy you're marrying in ten days' time."

Chapter Two

Rafe stared at his fiancé, fighting against the panic rising within him. Her eyes showed no hint of recognition, her expression holding only alarm and a touch of pity.

Even now, with her head swathed in bandages, her hair in a limp braid, no makeup, and shadows under her eyes, she was still the most beautiful woman he'd ever seen. The day he'd asked her to marry him and she'd said yes, he'd felt as if he could conquer the world. He'd taken her back to his place and made love to her, not wanting to let her go, wanting to worship her for hours to show her how much he loved her.

And now she was looking at him as if she'd never seen him before in her life.

He glanced at Noelle, whose brow had furrowed. "Give her time," she said.

Time? They were getting married in ten days!

"Ms. Goldsmith," the doctor said cheerfully as he came into the room. "Good to see you awake."

Rafe stepped to the side to give him space, his head still spinning.

"Hello," Phoebe replied.

"I'm Dr. Pine," he said. "I'm guessing everyone here is relieved to see you awake. How are you feeling?"

"Better. Very tired, though."

"Yes, well, you've had a traumatic brain injury. It's going to take you a while to heal. Your body will want to rest a lot, so it can concentrate on mending." He placed his clipboard on the bed and came forward. "Let's take a look then." The nurse helped him remove the dressing on the back of Phoebe's head, and they spent a minute examining the wound.

Her family talked in low voices while this happened, but Rafe stayed at the bottom of the bed, watching the doctor work. Phoebe stared at

SERENITY WOODS

her hands, but every now and then her gaze flicked up to Rafe, lowering again as soon as he caught her eye.

"It's looking good." The doctor moved back to let the nurse change the dressing. "You might find there's been damage to some of the hair follicles, but I think you'll be able to style your hair over it, so it shouldn't notice too much."

"I don't care," Phoebe said. "I'm just glad to be here."

Rafe saw her sisters exchange a look and understood their puzzlement. Phoebe might not spend a long time on her makeup, but she always took time on her hair. Before the accident, she would have been horrified at the thought of losing any of it. His unease deepened, but he scolded himself for it. Traumatic events like this were bound to change a person.

But how else might she have changed?

"Now, the nurse tells me you're having some trouble with your memory." The doctor picked up his clipboard.

She gave a little nod.

"You can't remember the accident?"

A little shake.

"What's the last thing you remember?"

She looked straight at the doctor, not glancing at the others around her. "Going to university."

Rafe's eyebrows rose. "What?"

"That was in 2010," Noelle pointed out to the doctor.

Elliot's jaw had dropped. "Jesus. You've lost eight years?"

"She doesn't remember anything after that." Noelle looked at Rafe.

This was more than a brief failure to recognize his face. His fiancée didn't remember meeting him. She'd forgotten everything they'd been through. All the little signposts along the way—their first date, first kiss, the first time they'd slept together. She didn't remember making love with him at all. All those wonderful moments they'd shared.

Emotion welled up in him, fierce and powerful as a tsunami. Noelle saw it and sorrow crossed her features, but he couldn't bear to hear her sympathy. Turning, he walked out of the room and strode off down the corridor.

He ran down the stairs to the ground floor, and didn't stop running until he was out of the hospital and in the courtyard. Sinking onto a bench, he leaned forward, his elbows on his knees, and put his face in his hands as his chest heaved.

Holy fucking Christ. He felt a sweep of loss, as strong as if she'd died, because in many ways the old Phoebe had. The comfort that a long-term relationship brings, the pleasure of sharing your life with someone, of knowing them intimately; it had all vanished in an instant.

What was he going to do? He sat there, fighting with his emotion, taking deep breaths, trying to calm himself.

After about ten minutes, he heard the door open, and someone walked across the paving stones toward him and sat on the bench. It was Elliot, Phoebe's brother, and his good friend.

"Coffee?" Elliot handed him a cup. "It's shit, but it's hot."

Rafe gave a short laugh, took the cup, and sipped it. It *was* shit, but it grounded him, and some of the panic began to ebb away.

"Did the doctor say anything else?" he asked.

"He's asking her a lot of questions, like if she could remember what happened yesterday, and this morning. She can; it's the accident and the eight years before it that have gone A.W.O.L. It's called retrograde amnesia. It's often temporary."

"How long before her memory returns?"

"Could be days, weeks, or never. No way of telling."

"Jesus." Rafe blew out a long breath and looked up at the sky. How come the sun was shining? There should be thunder and lightning, meteors falling. Wasn't that what happened when the world ended? "I can't believe she doesn't remember me." He felt a twist of hurt deep inside. He knew it wasn't her fault, but he couldn't fight the feeling that it was somehow a rejection, a conscious choice of hers to push him away.

"I'm so sorry, man. I can only imagine how you're feeling. But all's not lost. The doctor says one way to treat it is to expose her to memories from the loss. He said it would be good for her to talk to you, and for you to remind her of things you've done, places you've been, that sort of thing."

Rafe nodded. "She's happy with that?"

"She wants to remember. Just... take it slow. You're a stranger to her at the moment. But hopefully it won't last long, and we'll all be laughing about this in a few days' time."

Rafe looked down at his hands. "I hope so."

"The doctor's examining her now. He sent us all out of the room. He called it a moderate traumatic brain injury. He said it can affect a person in hundreds of different ways—physically, emotionally... I guess we'll have to wait and see how it's affected her. Apparently, it's common to be able to remember how to do everyday things like walk, talk, or play an instrument, and to recall your childhood. It's newer memories that are more likely to vanish."

They'd been a couple for two years, but her brain considered Rafe a new memory. Ouch, that stung. All the times they'd shared, the intimate things they'd done, the passion they'd felt for each other, and he was less important to her than someone she would have met at eighteen.

Logically, he knew it wasn't like that. It didn't stop it hurting, though.

Rafe put his head back in his hands. The doctor had caught up with him earlier on the way to Phoebe's room. "I understand that you're Ms. Goldsmith's fiancé," he'd said.

"That's right," Rafe had replied.

"A brain injury can affect people in many ways. I'll run through possible symptoms in a minute with the family present, but I wanted to mention a few things to you alone."

Rafe had stopped walking. "What is it?"

"You need to be aware that it's not unusual for the injured person's sex life to change. Obviously, there may be physical problems resulting from the accident, but there can also be other issues. Changes in the libido aren't uncommon."

"You mean she might not want sex anymore?" Rafe had gone cold.

"Well, that's one possibility on a very wide spectrum. Sometimes, the libido can *in*crease. But changes in her ability to become aroused, or in how much she feels like sex might happen. Occasionally, it can affect a person's attitude socially to sex…"

"What do you mean?"

"Well, it's common for someone with a brain injury to behave sexually at inappropriate times. And it's also possible that she might experience reproductive issues, and have problems becoming pregnant."

The doctor's news had made him feel nauseous, but now, sitting in the garden with Elliot, Rafe knew that issues with their love life were the least of his problems.

"She'll remember you," Elliot said. "How could she not? She was crazy about you, bro."

"Was," Rafe repeated.

"Yeah, well, I didn't mean—"

Rafe waved a hand. "I know. But what if she doesn't get her memory back?"

Elliot blinked. "That's not going to happen."

"It might. We're supposed to be getting married in ten days."

Elliot blew out a breath. "Let's not panic about it yet. She might remember everything in an hour. Let's go up and find out how she's doing, and take it step by step."

Rafe nodded, because there wasn't really anything else he could do.

Together, they walked back into the hospital and up the stairs to the first floor. When they got to Phoebe's room, she was alone, still on top of the covers, her eyes closed. The two guys surveyed her for a moment.

Rafe's throat tightened. On Thursday evening, after he'd finished his day shift, they'd had the most terrible argument. Upset and angry, Phoebe had shoved her feet in her running shoes and walked out, stating that she needed to run for a while. He should have stopped her and told her to stay with him so they could work it out, but he'd been frustrated and furious. He'd let her go, and now he'd always have that on his conscience.

When the police had turned up on his doorstep around eight p.m. to inform him she'd had an accident, Rafe had driven to the hospital far too fast, and had probably gained himself several speeding tickets on the way, not that he cared. He'd stayed by her side once she'd come out of surgery, refusing to leave all day Friday. Early on Saturday morning, Dominic had finally persuaded him to go home to catch a few hours' sleep and have a shower. He'd done so reluctantly, only to receive a phone call not long after he'd arrived home that she'd finally woken. He was angry with himself for leaving; he'd wanted to be the first person she saw when she woke up. As it happened, it was probably best that he hadn't been there, as she wouldn't have recognized him anyway.

He guessed it was karma, Fate's way of paying him back for letting her leave. It was so fucking cruel. Whatever had happened between them, neither of them deserved this.

"Let's find the others." Elliot tugged his sleeve. Tearing his gaze away from her face, Rafe followed him along to the TV room with a heavy heart.

Noelle, Roberta, and Bianca were the only ones in there, talking quietly. The two guys joined them, sitting on one of the sofas.

"You okay?" Bianca asked him.

He nodded. In his role as a firefighter, Rafe had met Elliot, who was a cop, several years ago through work when they'd both attended a coach crash on the state highway. Through Elliot, a few months' later, he'd met Phoebe, and had immediately fallen for the gorgeous blonde. He'd met her twin just days later, and he had to admit he'd been taken aback to meet someone who was the mirror image of the woman of his dreams. Back then, the two young women had possessed similar temperaments, both relatively quiet and gentle, with a wry sense of humor he loved. Phoebe had changed a lot since then, though. It had been one of the things that had come up in their argument on the day of the accident. An argument she no longer remembered. He wasn't sure how to feel about that.

"You look awful," Roberta said. Eighteen months older than the twins, she had a feistier temperament and a blunt way of speaking that he sometimes liked and sometimes found frustrating.

"Thanks." He shot her a glare.

"What was the doctor's verdict?" Elliot asked.

"He examined her all over," Noelle told them. "All things considered, it could have been a lot worse, physically. No broken bones, just a few bumps and bruises on her arms and legs and that graze on her hip. He said the head wound is doing well, and shows no signs of infection. He thinks he got all the little bits of gravel out of it, and it's already on the mend."

"What about the injury to her brain?" Rafe said.

"He spoke to her for a while, testing her speech, her reactions, her senses. Mostly, she seems fairly normal, which is good news. She's a little confused, which is to be expected if she's lost her memory. It's taking time to process her thoughts, but he hopes that will get better."

"And her memory?"

"She can remember a few moments following the accident, and what happened this morning. That might not seem like much, but it means she's laying down new memories, which is a good thing. But I know it's her long-term memory you're worried about. The thing is, there's no telling if or when it will return. Or even how badly her injury will affect her. She's going to be tired for a while, and she's going to need time to heal. He said to expect at the minimum some of the signs of PTSD."

"Like?" Rafe asked.

"Sleeping too much or not being able to get to sleep. Bad dreams. Anxiety or depression, especially when she can't remember something, or she encounters something that confuses her, such as technology she doesn't remember. Personality changes. There's a list as long as your arm of things that could happen, but it doesn't mean that all—or any— of them will. We're just going to have to wait and see how it goes. Dr. Pine said one way to help is to remind her of the memories she's lost, and that might trigger them to come back."

Rafe nodded and swallowed hard. Nobody was going to be able to reassure him that his fiancée would remember who he was today, tomorrow, or in six months' time. Or ever. Jesus. How was he going to deal with that?

"Until then," Noelle said, "I don't think we should tell her about what happened with her father."

Rafe exchanged a look with Elliot and the girls, then brought his gaze back to Phoebe's mother. "You want me to lie to her?"

"I would just like you to avoid giving her the details as long as you can. You know what kind of effect it had on her last time. Let's try to put that off for a while and let her heal."

His stomach churned uneasily. He had no secrets from his fiancée, and the notion of keeping things from her didn't sit well, even if Noelle thought it was for her benefit.

"How long is she going to have to stay in hospital?" Elliot asked.

"The doctor wants her to stay tonight, and then he'll see how she's feeling tomorrow. Providing her headaches are manageable, he said there's no real reason she can't go home to recover. They need the beds, I think, and she's out of immediate danger. But she'll have to have regular checkups with our GP for a while."

"Are you going to call off the wedding?" Roberta asked.

Rafe went cold. He hadn't even thought about it.

Elliot cleared his throat. "Let's talk about that later."

"I've been thinking," Noelle said softly. "I'd like Phoebe to come and stay with me for a while."

Rafe's heart skipped a beat, then gave a big thump against his ribs. "All her stuff is at the house," he said. "And if it's going to help to remind her of the memories she's lost, wouldn't it make sense for her to be in the place she's lived for the last six months?"

"She's going to need a certain amount of physical care," Noelle said. "You're not going to be able to take too much time off work." Her gaze was steady, her voice firm.

"I have four days off now," he snapped. "Her place is with me."

"She doesn't remember you," Noelle said. "You're a stranger to her. She needs her family around her right now."

His hands had tightened into fists without him realizing. He leaned forward, his elbows on his knees, and linked his fingers, trying to relax. He liked Noelle, had found in her the mother he'd lost when he was a little boy. She was ten times the woman his stepmother was. He didn't want to be rude or disrespectful. But at that moment, he felt as if they were two captains in Star Trek, brought onto one ship. Who had authority here? Noelle was Phoebe's mother, but he was her fiancé. Even if Phoebe didn't remember him, that ought to earn him some points, surely?

And yet, he wasn't her husband, not yet. Noelle was right; to Phoebe, he was a stranger.

But that didn't mean he was going to roll over and give in. His jaw was knotted so hard that his teeth hurt. "She's coming home with me," he said flatly.

"Maybe we should let Phoebe decide," Bianca said.

Rafe glanced at her. That made sense, except… he was afraid that Phoebe wouldn't choose him.

"She wanted to talk to you." Noelle's expression softened. "When she wakes. Why don't you spend some time with her? Bianca's right; it makes sense to let her choose. If she says she wants to stay with you, I won't argue, I promise. I only want what's best for her."

Rafe nodded and got to his feet. "I'll sit in with her so someone's with her when she wakes up."

Noelle stood too. "You've been amazing, sweetheart. I'm so glad she's got you. Whatever happens with her memory, she's still the same woman you fell in love with."

But was she? Noelle had mentioned personality changes as one possible effect of Phoebe's injury. Jesus. He couldn't process this right now.

"We'd better get back to the shop," Roberta said to her sister. "Libby's been great, but there are deliveries and stuff we need to check on."

Bianca nodded, and the two women said goodbye and left. "I'll take you home if you like," Elliot said to his mother. "I can always bring you back later if you want."

Noelle picked up her purse. "Okay. I could do with a few hours' sleep and a shower." She stopped by Rafe. "Take it slowly with her, eh?"

"I will." He nodded at Elliot, and watched the two of them walk away.

After fetching himself a soda from the vending machine in the foyer, he took it into Phoebe's room. She was still asleep.

He looked down at her for a long moment, tempted to lean forward and press his lips to hers. His heart ached at the memory of the argument they'd had before she'd walked out. He hadn't told anyone about it. He'd regretted it as soon as she'd left, and after the police had visited, he'd felt sick at the thought that he might never be able to apologize.

There was no point in apologizing now, not when she couldn't remember it. Maybe that was the silver lining to this thick gray cloud. In a way, he had a second chance to make this right before she remembered what had happened.

If she remembered.

Sighing, he sat in the chair under the window, and waited for her to wake up.

Chapter Three

This time when Phoebe opened her eyes, the first thing she saw was Rafe Masters sitting in a chair beneath the window. She blinked a few times, then realized she wasn't dreaming and he really was there, watching her.

Her first thought was that it was creepy for a stranger to watch her sleep. Then she reminded herself that, in his eyes, she wasn't a stranger. This man was her fiancé. She'd agreed to spend the rest of her life with him. To share herself with him in every possible way.

Holy moly.

He gave a small smile. "Hey. How are you feeling?"

"Better." Her headache had shrunk to a dull throb, and she ached less than she had when she'd first woken up that morning.

For a moment, though, she didn't move, just lay there studying him. The door was open, and she could hear the sounds of the hospital outside, nurses calling to one another, beds being wheeled, people coming and going. But in her room, it was quiet, and she welcomed the chance to let her body adjust to being awake, and to take the opportunity to examine this man in more detail.

Rafe bore her scrutiny patiently, not seeming to mind as her gaze slid down him, taking in the smaller details now they were alone. He really was extremely good looking. He hadn't shaved for a few days, and stubble darkened his jaw. He had a straight nose and the brightest blue eyes that held a wicked twinkle. He sat leaning back in the chair, his hands in the pockets of his jeans, knees wide the way all men sit. The denim stretched tight over impressive thighs.

Her gaze returned to his face. His small smile had reappeared.

"You need to brush your hair," she said.

He gave a short laugh and extracted a hand to run through it. "Yeah, well, when your fiancée is at death's door, bringing a hair brush is the last thing on your mind."

"Mum told me you sat here for thirty hours straight," she said softly. "You refused to leave."

He shrugged. "And then I missed you waking up." He rolled his eyes.

"I think it was probably for the best. It wasn't a pretty sight."

"I doubt that," he said. "You look gorgeous."

She snorted. "Even with the mummified bandages?"

"Even with."

He seemed serious. She didn't know what to say to that. If he'd been a stranger, she would have criticized him for cheesy chat up lines. But he wasn't. How on earth was she going to handle this?

"Where's your ring?" he asked.

"What ring?"

"Your engagement ring."

She blinked.

"They must have taken it off you when they brought you in." He got up, opened the drawer beside her bed, and took out a small purse which was presumably hers. She watched him open it, biting her lip at the urge to complain as this stranger rifled through her things.

"Here it is." He took out a ring and offered it to her on his palm.

She stared at it.

He lowered his hand slowly. "Shit," he said, "I didn't think. You don't remember it. I'm sorry. You don't have to wear it."

"No, it's okay." She reached out and took it from his palm.

The plain gold band was topped by seven shimmering diamonds in a Lotus shape. The total diamond weight must have been well over a carat.

"It's beautiful," she whispered, turning it around in her fingers.

"Got it out of a Christmas cracker," he said.

"No you did not," she scolded, throwing him a wry look. "This must be worth a fortune. How much did it cost?"

"You're not supposed to ask me that."

She'd heard that an engagement ring should cost two months' wages. She had no idea what he did for a living, but, unless he was very rich, she suspected that was a vast understatement.

She slid it on her ring finger. It fit perfectly, although it felt alien. She could remember as a teen going through her mother's rings with her sisters, trying them on and imagining what it would be like to wear her own one day, and now she really was getting married.

Holy shit. She wasn't going to think about it right now.

"Where's everyone else?" she asked.

"Your sisters have gone back to the shop. Elliot's taken your mum home for a sleep and a shower. She'll be back later. I don't know if you remember, but the doctor said it's good to talk about missing memories, to help encourage them back again."

"I remember."

"So, I thought you might want to chat for a while. How are you feeling? Fancy breaking out?"

Her eyebrows rose. "Of the hospital? The doctor said I should stay another night."

"Nah. I meant down to the cafe for a latte."

She realized she wanted a coffee more than anything else in the world. "I'd love one."

"Come on, then." He got to his feet and came around the bed as she sat up. "Do you want me to get a wheelchair?"

"No, no, I can walk." Someone had left a pair of ballet slippers by the side of the bed, and she slipped her feet into them. "Um… do I look presentable?" She was only wearing the T-shirt and track pants. She didn't even have a bra on underneath.

"You look great." He offered her his arm.

Phoebe stared at him. He looked taller and bigger standing right next to her. She'd been dating this man, had pledged to spend the rest of her life with him. This was so weird. She glanced up, and a tingle ran down her back as his blue eyes looked into hers. The poor guy. It wasn't his fault that she didn't know him from Adam.

"Just so you don't fall over," he said, gesturing with his arm again.

She took it, saying nothing, and together they left the room. She tried not to squeeze his biceps as they walked along the corridor.

"Feeling all right?" he asked. "Not dizzy or anything?"

"No. I'm okay." She was a little light-headed and weak, and her head still throbbed, but she had the feeling she'd been very lucky. A car had driven into her; she really could have been in a wheelchair for the rest of her life.

They got to the elevator, went in, and he pressed the button for the ground floor. The doors slid shut.

"I'm so sorry," she said as the carriage descended. "This must be awful for you."

"It's not your fault."

"I know. But I feel… responsible, I suppose, for not being able to remember you. You must be so upset."

He studied his feet. "I admit it was a bit hard to hear."

"How long have we known each other?"

"Just over two years. I asked your dad if I could marry you only a week before he died."

She felt a deep twist inside her at the reminder that she'd lost her father. She hadn't dealt with it properly yet. She'd try to process that devastating information when she was alone, because she knew she was going to bawl her eyes out. "I still can't believe he's gone," she admitted, her voice a little husky. "I feel as if I saw him yesterday."

"It was tough for you the first time, and it's harsh that you have to grieve all over again. It's a lot for you to deal with, on top of the accident."

The doors slid open, and he led her out into the foyer and along the corridor.

"That's true," she said, "but I have to count my blessings. I suppose I could have died in that accident. And I have a supportive family, which is more than many people have."

"And you have me," he said, opening the door of the cafe, and standing back to let her through.

She didn't reply, slipping past him, conscious of her arm brushing his chest. *Ohhh…* this was so weird. Part of her wished her mother or sisters had stayed so that she didn't have to be alone with him. But that was silly. He was her fiancé, and he deserved to spend some time with her, and to talk about where they went from here.

"So, latte?" he asked, leading her across to a table.

She sank into a chair gratefully. "Please."

"Would you like anything to eat?"

Her stomach rumbled. "Sure. You choose me something."

She watched him for a moment as he went up to the cabinets, and then she glanced around the room, at the other customers. One was reading a newspaper; a couple were looking at mobile phones. Several others were studying tiny screens about the size of a large book. What were they? Mini laptops?

Unease slid down her back like an ice cube. She felt like an alien who'd landed on an unfamiliar planet. She didn't just have her own life to worry about; she had to find out what had been happening in the world in general. She'd missed so much! Jesus, where did she start?

"You okay?" Rafe took the seat opposite her.

She nodded, swallowing hard, breathing through the wave of panic. "Just thinking about how much I must have lost. Have there been any world wars? Any world-wide catastrophes?"

"No, nothing like that. I'm going to have to brush up on my current events though, to bring you up to speed." He smiled, then reached out a hand to cover hers when she didn't return it. "Don't worry. We'll take it a step at a time. I'll be here to help."

She looked at their hands for a moment, then sat back and withdrew hers.

Rafe didn't comment on it. He just blew out a breath. "It's warm in here." Grabbing hold of his hoodie by the back of the neck, he tugged it over his head.

Phoebe watched as the gray tee he wore underneath rose with the hoodie, exposing a few inches of tanned skin, with an impressive ripple of stomach muscles. He dropped the hoodie and tugged the tee down, ran a hand through the hair that was still sticking up, and then grinned at the look on her face.

"It's all yours," he said, brushing his fingers down himself and then flicking them toward her as if to say, *Ta-da!*

Her face warmed. How on earth had she landed such a gorgeous guy? He drew the eyes of all the women in the room, although he seemed unaware of their gazes on him.

"So, we've been engaged a year?" she clarified.

"Yes."

She sucked her bottom lip for a moment, thinking about that tanned stomach, her gaze settling on his mouth. "And… we've been… intimate?" She lifted her gaze back to his.

His lips curved up. "Once or twice." The impish glint in his eyes told her it was a lot more than that. It didn't surprise her. Why would anyone ever want to get out of bed if they were with this man?

His gaze had slid to her mouth, and she knew he was thinking about kissing her, maybe even what she looked like naked. And yet she didn't remember sleeping with him; she didn't remember any intimate moments at all. As gorgeous as he was, she shivered at the thought of undressing in front of a stranger. Had she had any one-night stands? Had she even slept with anyone else?

"It's so odd," she whispered. "You imply I'm not a virgin, but I feel like one. Were you my first?"

"No. You'd had two partners before me." He spoke with confidence that she hadn't kept any secrets from him.

She'd shared herself in the most intimate way with two other men. Would she ever recall their faces?

The waitress came over with their lattes, then returned with two plates of sandwiches. One had slices of roast beef; the other looked like it was all salad.

She pulled the beef one toward her and took a big bite out of it.

It was only once she'd swallowed it and went to take a second mouthful that she realized Rafe was staring at her.

She stopped mid-bite and said, "What?"

"Nothing."

"Rafe…"

"That was mine. You're vegetarian."

Her eyes widened. "You're kidding me."

"No."

"I don't eat meat anymore?"

"Not for about ten months."

"Holy shit." She stared at the sandwich, then shrugged and ate it. "I might as well make the most of the amnesia, then."

It was a flippant comment, but her heart raced. Not only did she not recognize Rafe, she didn't recognize herself. This was like something out of a sci-fi movie.

He looked at the salad sandwich, gave a little sigh, then took a bite.

"Why am I vegetarian?" she asked, thinking how lovely the beef tasted.

"You gave up meat when you started running. You said it sat for too long in the stomach."

"Do I run a lot?"

He gave a short laugh that she wasn't sure held a lot of humor. "Yeah, you could say that."

"Mum said I was doing a triathlon."

"Yeah, next month."

"Jesus. It doesn't sound like me. Did I have a personality transplant?"

He sipped his coffee, keeping his gaze on his cup. "You changed a lot after your father died. It was as if his death made you want to cram as much into every day as you could, and you wanted to help other people. You raise a lot of money for the Heart Foundation."

She blew out a long breath. It was as if he was talking about someone else.

"Let's start by talking about you," she said.

"Okay." He had another bite of the sandwich.

"How old are you?" she asked.

"Twenty-nine."

"Siblings?"

"Two brothers, Ben, who's older, and Josh, who's younger. You've met them. You thought Ben was pompous and Josh was cute. I sulked at that, and it made you laugh."

She smiled. He was obviously used to teasing her. She liked that. "Are your parents alive?"

"My mum died when I was three. Dad then married the Wicked Witch of the Northland. Don't laugh, she really is. We've clashed since day one. I left home as soon as I could and lived with Ben for a while before I went to Rotorua to train as a firefighter."

"You're a firefighter?"

"Yeah. I'm a Senior Firefighter at Kerikeri Fire Station."

Oh jeez. The thought of him in uniform made her feel lightheaded again.

She finished off the sandwich and licked her fingers. "So… tell me about yourself."

He shrugged. "I'm a Kiwi guy. I like fishing and surfing and hanging out with my friends and family. I have no great aspirations to conquer the world."

"Do we live together?"

"Yes. We bought a house together and moved in about six months ago. It's a smallish, two-bedroomed place overlooking the inlet."

"Are we happy?" she asked softly.

His gaze drifted away, and she knew he was remembering scenes from their life together. What images was he seeing? It was as if he'd been to the premiere of a movie she really wanted to see.

"We were very happy," he said.

"Past tense?"

His gaze came back to her. "I don't want to assume."

She lowered her eyes and picked at the lid of the coffee cup. He was aware, at least, that slipping straight back into their old relationship was unlikely to happen. She was pleased about that.

"So… we're supposed to get married in ten days," she said. "Tell me about that."

"We'll be married at two o'clock on Valentine's Day, in the grounds of a small hotel in Paihia. Dominic will marry us, and then we'll—"

"Wait, what?"

"He's a deacon," Rafe said. "Although he'll be there just as a celebrant, not with his religious hat on."

Phoebe's jaw dropped. "He's been *ordained?*"

"Yep. Some years now."

"Is he going to be a priest?"

"No, he's chosen to be a vocational deacon—he's a qualified counsellor too, at the high school. But he can marry us."

Phoebe had trouble processing that. "We've never been a religious family. What made him do that?"

"A woman," Rafe said, and smiled.

"Jo," she said softly. "Of course." Dominic had started seeing her when he was eighteen, and they'd married at twenty-one. Jo was sweet and gentle, and Phoebe liked her a lot. She'd known Jo was religious, although Jo hadn't been overt about it. "So she converted him?"

"Something like that. He says she introduced him to his calling. They had a baby, a girl, called Emily—she's seven now. And then…" Rafe's brow furrowed. "Unfortunately, and I'm sorry to tell you this, Jo died, about two years ago now, just before I met you."

"Oh no." Phoebe stared at him in shock. "How?"

"She had an asthma attack, of all things. Dominic took it real hard, and I think it challenged his faith. But he seems to be through the worst."

Phoebe head was starting to hurt again. It was as if trying to stuff new details back into her brain caused it pain.

"You look a bit pale," Rafe said. "Do you want to go back to your room?"

"No, I'm okay. It's just a bit of a shock to realize how much has changed. I mean, we all know the world moves on without us once we're gone. It's just odd coming back and realizing that. Has anyone else close to me died?"

Pity crossed his face. "No, sweetheart, that's it."

She chewed her bottom lip. She was going to have to ask him about her own history now. The thought made her nervous—what had she done, where had she been? She already knew she'd turned vegetarian, and that she ran a lot. What if she didn't like the new her? What would she do then?

She cleared her throat. "Okay. So, give me a summary of the last eight years of my life."

Chapter Four

Rafe took a mouthful of his coffee and surveyed Phoebe thoughtfully. She looked nervous. He didn't blame her. He couldn't even begin to imagine how difficult this was for her.

She still looked the same, bar the bandages and the pale face. But the fact that she'd eaten the beef sandwich had shocked him. She wasn't the same woman who'd left the house on Thursday evening. He felt as if he didn't know the person sitting opposite him at all.

But that was idiotic, because she was still Phoebe, his fiancée. Still the girl who'd once told him that he was the man of her dreams, and who'd sighed his name in the darkness after they'd made love. It was his job to help her remember that.

"I'll start at the beginning," he said. "You went to university at eighteen."

"I took a fashion and textiles course, right?"

"Yep. You and Bianca. She made clothes and you did beadwork and embroidery on them."

"I remember that. We used to spend hours sewing when we were kids. Mum loved needlework, and she used to buy us patterns and material to practice with."

"Well, in your second year at uni you made a whole range of dolls of Henry VIII and his six wives with detailed medieval gowns. They won a special award. Auckland Museum bought them, and they're on display as part of their medieval section."

"Holy shit!" She looked genuinely shocked.

He smiled. "Cool, eh? You took me there to show me them—they're amazing. They must have taken you hundreds of hours. Anyway, your interest turned to wedding dresses. In the final year of your degree, Bianca designed and sewed a fantasy-style gown based on the elven dresses from *The Lord of the Rings* movie, and you did all the embroidery and beadwork on it. The university thought it was good enough to enter into the World of Wearable Arts competition, and you ended up winning the Student Innovation Award."

Her jaw dropped. "Oh my God."

"Once you'd graduated, you both had several offers for jobs across the country. But you'd been talking for a while about setting up a bridal shop up here. You were both home birds, and neither of you really wanted to move away. Your parents had some savings that they offered to invest in the shop. So, you opened the Bay of Islands Brides."

"Oh, really?"

"In the middle of Kerikeri. It's very popular. You have a sewing room out the back where you make the dresses. You sell other brands too, but many people come to the shop just for your gowns. Your mum runs the shop. After the first year, you bought the shop next door and knocked down the wall in between, and turned it into a cafe. Roberta runs it. People can sit and have a drink and a muffin while Noelle shows them the dresses. You all work late on Thursdays and have special evenings where volunteers come in and model the gowns, like a fashion show. They're always well attended."

"It sounds amazing."

"It's done very well." He hesitated. "Things are changing a bit now, though."

"In what way?"

He scratched at a mark on the lid of his cup. "In a few months' time, we're moving to Auckland."

Her eyebrows rose. "Really?"

"I got a promotion at a fire station there, to Station Officer. And you're going to work at Mackenzie's—it's a huge bridal shop on Queen Street."

Phoebe looked puzzled. "I'm leaving the shop here?"

"Well, the idea is that you come back at weekends and catch up on some of the work then."

"That doesn't sound ideal," she said.

He shrugged, not sure what to say.

"Are you excited about your promotion?" she wanted to know.

"Of course," he said.

"What does my family think about me moving?"

"They're pleased for you, but disappointed too, obviously. You have a friend, Libby, who's going to fill in for your turns in the shop during the week. But she can't fill in for the needlework, obviously."

"What does Bianca think?"

He had a mouthful of coffee, not sure how to tell her about her twin's bitter disappointment. "You've worked together a long time, and of course you're twins. She's finding it hard. But she'll manage. The two of you can't be joined at the hip forever."

Phoebe narrowed her eyes. "Why do I have the feeling you're hiding something from me?"

"I don't know." He sipped his coffee again.

"I don't understand why I'd leave the bridal shop here. And what about all the running, and the triathlon? It's odd, it seems like I just changed dramatically. Was it all to do with my father passing away?"

"Yes. It had a profound effect on you. You began to talk about how you had to make the most of every day, and how you felt you were wasting time staying in Kerikeri. You were quite curvy when I met you. But you went on a major health kick, turned vegetarian, started running, and it just went on from there. You trained for the half marathon first. Then you bought a bike and you were cycling everywhere. And you swim every day in your mum's pool."

"I don't associate with that person at all," she whispered. "It's so odd."

He shifted in his seat. "Well, you can't remember the shock of your father passing. I mean, I know it's a shock now, but of course at the time everyone was there, and your mum was upset, and the whole event was traumatic. It was hard for you."

Her eyes had turned glassy, but she blinked the tears away and swallowed. "I don't want to talk about that."

"Okay."

"I just mean that I need to think about that when I'm on my own."

"It's okay, I understand.'

She nodded. "So… what about us?"

"What do you want to know?"

"Where did we meet?"

"I met Elliot through work, got to know him, and then he introduced us."

"What does Elliot do?"

"He's a cop."

She laughed. "He's the last person I would've thought would be a police officer."

"He's a damn good one, actually."

She nodded, amusement lighting her face for a moment. "So… we started dating."

"Yep. Took me a year to convince you to marry me." He smiled.

"So, the wedding's booked for the fourteenth."

"Yes. And then we're going to Fiji for five days for our honeymoon. We've been looking forward to it for a long time," he said. "Hot weather. Lying by the pool. Long warm nights in our room." He winked at her.

She didn't smile back.

Instead, she surveyed him for a while. Rafe let her, even though inside his heart was hammering. There was of course so much more to tell her, but he didn't want to overwhelm her.

"Do we want kids?" she asked.

He finished off his coffee. This was so hard. He should tell her everything, lay it all out on the table. But it was unfair to push his agenda when she didn't remember the reasons for the decisions they'd made. It was possible her memory would return, and if it did, no doubt she would have a strong opinion on how he handled these next few days.

"We've talked about it," he said. "But what with my promotion and your new job, it doesn't seem like the right time. We thought maybe in a few years."

"Do we… um… use condoms?"

"Ah, no. You have an IUD fitted."

Her pale face turned pink.

"Sorry," he said. "You did ask."

"It's just so weird. You know the most intimate things about me, and I can't remember any of it. You could tell me anything, and how would I know if it was true? You're a complete stranger to me, and I just have to trust everything you say."

He sat up a bit. "I know this isn't easy for you."

"No offence, but I don't think you have the first idea how I feel. How could you? Imagine a woman walking up to you right now, a woman you've never met before, who tells you the most intimate details about the two of you together."

He studied his hands. There was nothing he could say to make this easier for her.

"I know it's not your fault," she said, a note of desperation in her voice, "and I'm sorry if I'm being harsh. This must be difficult for you, too. I don't know how to deal with it."

"Well," he said, "there are two ways. Your mum wants you to move back in with her for a while, so she can look after you. So, you could do that. We could cancel the wedding, and wait for your memory to come back."

"What if it doesn't?"

He didn't say anything.

"What's option two?" she asked.

"You could come home with me," he said softly. "And you could give me ten days to convince you to marry me on Valentine's Day."

They looked at each other for a long moment.

"I'm not trying to push you," he said eventually. "I'd sleep on the couch, if you wanted. I've got four days off now—I'm not back on shift until the ninth, so I'll be close by if you're not feeling well. Over the next ten days, I'll take you on a tour of our past. We'll go back to where we had our first date, where we first kissed. Places that are important to us. And maybe that will help you remember."

And if it didn't, he thought, it would give him ten days to make her fall in love with him all over again.

"What if we get to the wedding and I can't go through with it?" she said.

"That's not going to happen."

She gave a short laugh. "You're very sure of yourself."

"I'm sure of us." Anger flared inside him at the thought of what Fate had done to them almost on the eve of their wedding. He leaned forward, resting his forearms on the table. "You agreed to be my wife. I'm not going to just sit back and let that slip away from me. Do you think you would have said you'd marry me if you weren't in love with me? I'm crazy about you. And you're crazy about me, even if you don't know it yet."

Her eyes widened, but he hadn't finished. He had to get this off his chest.

"I won't go into details right now," he continued, "because I think you've had enough to deal with for one day. But over the next ten days, I'm not going to hold back. I'm going to remind you of every little detail of our relationship and how we feel about each other. We have sex most nights, Phoebe, often more than once. In every position and every way possible. You're the sexiest girl I've ever met, and I'm head over heels in love with you. You think I'm just going to roll over and give up on that because this is tough for you? Well, I'm not. The Phoebe I love would want me to fight for her, so that's what I'm going to do."

He was going all-in, taking the risk that he might frighten her off, banking on the fact that, deep inside, some part of her heart remembered the connection they'd had.

He waited, breathless with fear that he'd said too much.

She looked completely bemused. Gradually, though, her lips curved up, and humor lit her eyes.

"Wow," she said. "Is that you putting your foot down?"

He leaned back in the chair and gave her a wry look. "Maybe."

"It's quite impressive."

"Don't mock me. I'm in ten kinds of torment here."

Her expression softened. "I know. And I'm sorry. But you have to understand that I can't give you any kind of promise. If the wedding had been booked for tomorrow, I would have to cancel it. I can't marry a man I don't know. It's just too weird. But it's possible my memory might come back over the next week. If it does, and if I still feel the same way, then I guess we'll be getting married on Valentine's Day."

If I still feel the same way. Rafe looked out of the window, across the courtyard to where he'd sat with Elliot that morning. He should be honest and tell her everything. But if he did that, she would undoubtedly cancel the wedding, and he would lose the one woman he'd ever loved.

He'd wait, he decided, for a few more days. He couldn't believe her memory would be gone forever. No doubt as he introduced her to places they'd been, she'd gradually begin to remember, and then she'd be able to make her own decision as to their future. And if she didn't remember, he'd make sure that before the big day he revealed the events of the previous week, so she could make an honest decision.

He'd give himself a week to win her heart again. And hopefully by then, even if her memory did come back, she wouldn't be able to let him go.

Chapter Five

Phoebe's heart was still racing five minutes later, when Rafe led her back to her room. Tiredness overwhelmed her, but even after he'd taken his seat under the window to read and she'd closed her eyes, his words continued to flitter around in her head like butterflies.

We have sex most nights, Phoebe, often more than once. In every position and every way possible.

She was torn between longing and panic. She couldn't deny she found him sexy. Of *course* she did; he was gorgeous. She'd lost her memory, not her whole brain. In fact, secretly, she was impressed with her choice of groom. Things would have been a million times worse if she'd woken to discover she was engaged to the Hunchback of Notre Dame.

And yet… Somehow, it made things harder, too. She'd been a virgin when she'd gone to university at eighteen, both she and Bianca having been the type of shy girls who concentrated on their school work. She didn't remember being intimate with him—with any man, in fact. Just the thought of getting naked with a guy, especially such a gorgeous one, made her want to hyperventilate into a paper bag.

Keeping her eyes closed, she shifted onto her side facing the window and settled down. She waited for about thirty seconds, then opened her eyes.

Rafe was looking at one of the little screens that she'd seen people reading in the cafe. The sunlight glinted off his dark brown hair, highlighting it with gold. He hadn't put his hoodie back on, and the tee stretched across impressive shoulders, the sleeves tight around his biceps. If he was a firefighter, he'd have to work out regularly—that would explain the muscles, and the easy way he moved, as if he was confident with his body. He had a restless energy she liked; no doubt he had trouble sitting still for long. Although, apparently, he had sat by her side for thirty hours straight. That made her feel warm and fuzzy inside.

Yes, she liked him. But enough to marry him? How could she possibly stand opposite him and swear she was going to love him forever when she had no memory of their relationship? It was like an arranged marriage, and even though it happened in various cultures across the world, for her getting married was something you did with someone you trusted and loved.

He touched the screen he was holding and started tapping as if he was typing on a keyboard. She watched him, wondering if she was being stupid. Other women would kill for the chance to be Rafe Masters' wife, she was sure. If it came to it and her memory didn't return, was she really going to refuse to say "I do"? He seemed kind and gentle, and yet sexy enough to ensure a girl would never get bored in the bedroom. What was not to like?

He stopped typing, and then, without moving his head, he looked up at her. His lips curved up.

She decided it was pointless to be embarrassed at being caught staring. "What's that?" she said instead, gesturing at the tiny screen in his hand.

He looked puzzled, then obviously realized she didn't remember. "It's an iPad." He got to his feet, leaving it on the chair, came over to the bed, and retrieved a matching one from the cupboard. "This is yours." He handed it to her.

She shifted onto her back and turned it over in her hands, admiring how light it was. He pressed the button on the frame, and the screen came to life.

"I guess they must have first come out around 2010," he said. He logged her into the hospital wifi and explained what some of the apps were. "This is one of your most treasured possessions. It barely leaves your hands. Have a little explore." He returned to his seat, picked up his own tablet, and started to read again.

Phoebe looked at all the apps and opened the one for email. She appeared to have several email addresses, none of which was the one she'd used at uni. Touching each of them, she scanned through the unopened emails from the past few days. She had a business address, which was filled with emails from bridal magazines, sewing magazines, and several from Mackenzies, the shop where she'd gotten herself a new job, according to Rafe.

"Have you told Lisa Mackenzie that I had the accident?" she asked him after reading the woman's message that chatted away about how excited she was to have Phoebe coming to work for her.

"Yes, I rang her. She wants you to call when you feel up to it."

Phoebe returned her gaze to the iPad. At the moment, she wouldn't have a clue what to say.

She also had a personal address, and she flicked through those emails. Mainly from people she didn't know. She had a few from Roberta with funny pictures or chirpy little messages. Occasionally one from her mother or her brothers. Nothing from Bianca, though, which surprised her.

"How do Bianca and I keep in touch?" she asked Rafe.

"You see her every day," he said.

"I know, but we always used to email as well."

"Text or Facebook, I guess." He didn't look up.

Of course, Facebook. She brought up the Facebook app and had a look around the site. It was different from what she remembered, but easy enough to navigate. Some friends she recognized, others she didn't. There were lots of well wishes from people who'd obviously heard about her accident.

Still no messages from Bianca, though. Leaning over, she picked up the phone lying nearby and pressed the button on the side. It had a touch screen like the iPad.

"I don't suppose you know my password?" she asked Rafe.

He looked amused. "It's Henry8."

"I really got into the Tudors, then," she said wryly, not missing the fact that she'd obviously trusted him enough to tell him her password. "I remember the series."

"We've watched it, like, ten times."

Smiling, she typed it into the phone. It took her a moment to navigate to her messages. To her surprise, there was still nothing from Bianca.

She put down the phone and studied him.

His gaze rose slowly to meet hers. "What?" he said.

"What aren't you telling me?"

"I don't know what you mean."

"I can't remember, Rafe. It's not fair to hide things from me. If this is going to work, you need to be completely honest with me. I don't believe Bianca and I don't keep in touch when we're apart. What's happened?"

He ran a hand through his hair. "Fair enough. You had a bit of a tiff a few weeks ago."

Phoebe went cold inside. She'd been so close to her twin growing up, she'd sometimes felt as if they were the same person. They'd never argued as children or teens. To hear they'd done so now was as shocking as hearing she'd turned vegetarian. "What about? My new job?"

He nodded. "I think she saw it as a kind of betrayal, that you wanted to go on to better things."

She moved onto her side again, facing him. "Do you think she was right?"

He rubbed at the screen of his iPad with the sleeve of his hoodie. "I can see her point of view, but I don't think you should stay here just because of other people. You have to follow your heart."

She tucked her hands beneath her cheek, her eyelids drooping. He'd told her he'd been given a promotion at an Auckland fire station. She must have gotten the job at Mackenzie's to support him. If he'd really wanted to go, it would have been difficult to maintain a relationship if she'd stayed in Kerikeri, three-and-a-half hours away.

Maybe that friction was the reason that she sensed an unease in him. If he'd pushed her into moving, causing issues with her sister and the rest of her family, he might now feel guilty. He didn't want to admit it was his fault.

She understood, but if he wasn't being honest with her about that, what else might he be lying to her about?

He wanted her to trust him, but something wasn't right here. All she had until her memory returned were her instincts, and until she knew better, she was going to have to trust them.

*

She dozed for a couple of hours, and when she awoke, Rafe had gone and her mother was sitting in the chair. Noelle smiled as she saw that her daughter was awake, and she stood and came over to give her a kiss on the cheek.

"Where's Rafe?" Phoebe asked.

"Gone to get a coffee. He'll be back soon." Noelle perched on the bed. "How are you feeling?"

"A bit better each time I wake up. The headache's still there, though."

"The nurse left you these to take." Noelle passed her the pot of pills and a bottle of water. "Drink up. You don't want to get dehydrated."

Phoebe took the pills and downed a third of the bottle of water, then lay back with a sigh.

"You look pale still." Noelle stroked her cheek.

"I'm okay. Could have been a lot worse."

Noelle nodded. "Rafe told me that he's asked you to stay with him rather than come home with me."

"Mm."

"Have you decided what you want to do?"

"Not yet. I thought I might make my mind up in the morning."

"If you want to stay with me for a while, it's not a reflection on Rafe, or on the wedding, or anything except the fact that you've had a serious accident and you need time to recover."

"I know." Phoebe smiled as a porter came in wheeling a trolley full of trays of food.

"Dinner," he said cheerfully, and placed the tray on her table before disappearing.

She investigated the plate of food, discovering it was some kind of lentil stew. "It's vegetarian."

"You're vegetarian," Noelle said.

"Oh yeah, I forgot." She started eating the stew, thinking longingly of the beef sandwich Rafe had bought for her.

"I mentioned to him about postponing the wedding," Noelle said. "He told me he'd asked you not to."

"Yeah."

"That's not really fair. He shouldn't put pressure on you right now. Stress is the last thing you need."

"He wasn't pressurizing me. He just wants to marry me, that's all." Phoebe felt a need to defend him. Was that because part of her felt a connection with him? Remembered how close they used to be? Or just because she felt sorry for the guy who'd lost his fiancée?

"He said that Bianca and I had a tiff," she commented, "about me going to Auckland."

Noelle nodded slowly.

"Is she really against it?" Phoebe asked.

"She was surprised, that's all. We've spent a long time building the business. But we'll survive. We have a good deal of stock, and you'll be coming up at weekends to help out."

Phoebe still thought that sounded far from ideal. If she'd made the decision to take this job, she was sure she'd want to commit to it a hundred percent. And she'd be newly married to a husband who worked shifts; why would she want to spend her days off travelling and working? Guilt must have forced her into that decision. To have spent years building up the family business and then abandoning it… No wonder Bianca was angry with her. Without Phoebe to put the finishing touches to her gowns, the business would have to rely on selling other brands, which was fine, except that obviously wasn't why they'd created the shop.

She didn't say anything, though. She was going to try not to second guess herself. Who knew why she'd made the decisions she had? It was like trying to complete a one-thousand-piece jigsaw puzzle with only ten pieces—she had no hope of seeing the whole picture yet.

Finishing the lentil stew, she pushed it away and picked up the dish of fruit and custard. "Do you and Rafe get on okay?" she asked Noelle as she ate a few mouthfuls.

Her mother's eyebrows rose. "Of course! Why did you ask that?"

"I just wondered whether you liked him. I trust your judgment probably better than my own."

Noelle smiled and reached out to cup her cheek. "He's the best thing that ever happened to you. He adores you."

"And we've been okay leading up to the wedding?"

"I think there's been some tension between you. I just put it down to the stress of organizing everything."

"I'm looking forward to the wedding though?"

"Of course. You can't wait."

"And to my new job?"

"You seemed to be."

"Something doesn't feel right," Phoebe said softly. "But I've no way of knowing why. It's a horrible feeling. I just have to trust that everyone's being honest with me. It's easier with you and the others, but with Rafe… It's hard to trust someone who feels like a total stranger."

"It must be very difficult. All I can say is that before the accident, you would have trusted Rafe with your life."

"What sort of relationship do we have?" Phoebe wondered.

"Fiery." Noelle smiled. "He's not going to be easy to tame. He's irreverent and mischievous—I can only imagine what he was like as a boy. I bet he ran rings around his stepmother."

"Do we argue a lot?"

"Not argue… You've always been a good girl, followed the rules, done what's right. Rafe's not like that. He parks on double yellow lines. He's often late. He only thinks of today. I've seen him tease you until you're ready to scream, and then he laughs and kisses you, and you deflate like a soufflé in his arms. You're good for each other. You bring some order to his life and make him think about his actions. He tries to stop you being so serious."

"Doesn't sound like he's doing very well," Phoebe commented.

Noelle studied her thoughtfully. "You changed a lot after Dad died. It had a profound effect on you."

"Rafe said the same. Mum, I'm so sorry. I can't imagine how awful it's been for you." Her throat tightened.

But Noelle just held her hand and smiled. "It was difficult, but I had my family around me. And we had the shop, and that helped a lot, oddly. It was something to focus on, I suppose."

The shop had become a character in her own past, Phoebe thought. She would have to go and visit it, and see whether it jogged any memories.

"You seem very fond of it," she commented.

"We all worked very hard to get it off the ground. You and Bianca were sewing twelve hours a day, seven days a week, to make sure we had enough stock through those first few months. Roberta's done wonders with the cafe—it's one of the most popular places in town for women to come and have a gossip, even if they're already married! And Libby has brought her marketing expertise to us, and helped us with the shows, which have done wonders in getting the word out there. You remember Libby, right?"

"Of course. She was in Elliot's year at school."

"She's dating a friend of his now, Mike, another police officer. The four of them go out a lot."

"Is Elliot married then?"

"No, but he's been living with Karen for a few years."

"It's so odd," Phoebe whispered. "Everyone's moved on, but I feel as if I've been standing still. Except I haven't, of course."

"It'll come back to you," her mother reassured her.

Phoebe wasn't so sure. But she didn't say anything.

The nurse came in, checked her blood pressure and oxygen levels, and announced she was doing very well before leaving them to it.

Phoebe smiled as Rafe appeared at the door. "Hey."

He came in. "The cafe's closed. Foiled again."

"I suppose we should think about going now," Noelle said. "Let you get some rest."

"I've just woken up," Phoebe pointed out.

"You don't have to sleep, but you've had a lot to deal with today. I'm sure you need time to process it all."

It was true; she was already tired again. Rafe looked disappointed, but Phoebe nodded her assent that they could go.

"Have a think about what you want to do tomorrow," Noelle said, "and let us know."

"I will."

Noelle kissed her forehead. "I'm glad you're feeling better. It'll be good to get you home."

Rafe came up to her bedside and put a hand on hers. "See you tomorrow."

"See you," she said, her heart picking up speed at his touch.

He hesitated, then bent and kissed her cheek. Phoebe let him, glad he hadn't tried to kiss her mouth. A little bit of her wanted him to. But the bigger part knew she wasn't ready for that yet.

"I'll be here tomorrow morning, whatever you decide," he told her. "I'm so glad you're feeling better."

She nodded, and watched the two of them leave the room.

After visiting the bathroom, she slipped off her track pants and got into bed. Turning onto her side, she read her iPad for a while, trying to catch up on the world news over the past eight years. There was too much to read. Wars here, there, and everywhere. Tsunamis and earthquakes, including several in Christchurch that looked pretty bad. The usual scandals and political dramas. In the end, she put the pad down, not sure whether to feel disheartened or enlivened about the fact that the more things changed, the more they stayed the same.

Her phone beeped, and she picked it up and saw it was a text from Rafe. *Sleep well*, it said, and it finished with an x for a kiss.

Her lips curving up a little, she suddenly had an idea, and opened up the photos app. Sure enough, there were hundreds of photos, and she caught her breath as she scanned through them, slowly going back in time. There were lots of her family, of Bianca pulling a face, her mother laughing, of Elliot giving her a wry look as she asked him to pose for her. There were a couple of Dominic wearing his dog collar, which made her smile. She had the feeling she'd been very proud of him. Quite a few selfies of her in a vest and shorts after running some kind of marathon, her face red and sweaty, a look of triumph in her eyes. She hardly recognized herself.

Most of them were of Rafe, though. With friends in bars, smiling at the camera, holding up a drink. With two guys who were obviously his brothers, laughing. Some selfies she'd taken of the two of them, several with them kissing. And then one appeared of the two of them in bed, her holding the phone above their heads, laughing. Rafe's hand was under the covers—she could only imagine what he was doing down there. *We have sex most nights, Phoebe, often more than once. In every position and every way possible.* He was looking at the camera with a smug smile, as if he knew perfectly well how sexy he was. If she'd had any doubt before, she knew now that it was all true—they really were a couple who'd shared their lives in the most intimate way possible.

Her face burning, she flicked the photo away, and then inhaled sharply. It was a picture of her father, looking exactly how she remembered him, slightly plump, graying hair thinning on top, smiling self-consciously as she asked him to pose for her.

Turning off the phone, she put it on the table, then curled up and finally let herself think about the fact that he'd gone.

No longer would she be able to ring him and ask for his advice or help. She'd never be able to throw her arms around him again, and have that great bearhug he used to give, lifting her off the floor. She wouldn't be able to buy him birthday cards that teased him about his age or his weight.

The tears came, and she didn't fight them; she just lay there and let the emotion wash over her. It was harsh and painful, but if she were honest with herself, it wasn't as bad as she'd expected.

Deep down, did she remember grieving the first time? Were her memories still stored in her mind, as if they were filed away in trunks in a dusty attic? Maybe her very cells had memory, so that her bones and her muscles and skin stored information of all her past experiences.

Did that mean that deep inside was some memory of Rafe? Of the times they'd shared, of the feelings she'd had for him?

There was no way of knowing. She'd just have to wait and see how she felt from day to day, rather than try to make decisions right now.

Exhausted by the emotion of the day, she closed her eyes, but the touch of his lips on her cheek remained with her, even as she drifted off to sleep.

Chapter Six

When Rafe woke up at six-thirty and reached for his phone the way he did every morning, he discovered a text waiting for him from Phoebe.

I've given it a lot of thought, the message said. *And I've decided, I'd like to come home with you.*

That was all it said. Rafe read it, heart racing, barely able to believe his eyes. He'd gone to sleep convinced she'd choose to go with her mother.

He lowered the phone and turned his head to look at the space beside him on the bed. It had felt odd the last few nights being alone. He'd gotten used to having Phoebe beside him, to being able to reach out and touch her in the night. To hearing her around the house, singing.

He'd come so close to losing her. And not just because of the accident.

The last few weeks—maybe even months—had been hard. Did everyone's relationship feel strained in the lead up to a wedding? He guessed so. Not that he wasn't looking forward to marrying her, because he was enough of a man to feel a sense of smug possessiveness at the thought of putting a ring on her finger.

But there was no doubt that all the conversations they'd had about moving to Auckland had caused tension between them. Add to that the stress of organizing the wedding, and they'd been ripe for an explosion. The argument on Thursday hadn't been their first, but it had been their biggest, and it had upset them both. When she'd shoved on her running shoes and left the house, Rafe had punched the door to the bedroom so hard he'd put his fist through it.

He looked at the hole now, pursing his lips. Rising from the bed, he picked up a cinema poster they'd been given when they'd gone to the movies, collected some Blu-Tac, and stuck the poster over the hole.

He didn't want Phoebe to see it and start asking questions about that night. He'd raise the subject of their argument once she'd settled back in, and not before.

Suppressing unease that he was keeping yet another secret from her, he returned to the bed, rolled onto his front, and replied to her text.

<3<3<3 So pleased you're coming home. Can I come and get you now?

She replied within a minute. *Need to get everything signed and cleared first. They think probably mid-morning.*

I'll be leaving soon, he said. *Do you want me to bring your mum?*

She replied: *No, it's okay, I've let her know that you're picking me up.*

Cool, he said. *I'll see you soon, then. x*

He tossed the phone aside and leapt out of bed to get showered.

*

Just before eight-thirty, he pulled into the hospital car park and made his way up to the first floor.

He found Phoebe sitting in the chair beneath the window, looking at her iPad. Stopping in the doorway, he leaned against the doorjamb for a moment. She sucked her bottom lip as she read, playing with a strand of her hair. It had been less than a week since they'd last made love, but he felt a deep sense of longing to hold her in his arms again, to have her wrapped around him, her mouth on his as she arched her back to meet his thrusts. At that moment, when he was inside her and she was looking into his eyes, her own hazy with passion, he knew that she was his, and he felt as if they'd be together forever.

At that moment, she looked up and saw him standing there.

"You've got to stop doing that," she said.

He came into the room. "Doing what?"

"Watching me without me knowing. It creeps me out."

"You've got to get used to it. I do it a lot while you sleep."

"You do not," she protested, her face turning pink.

"All the time." He smiled. "How are you feeling?"

"I'm okay."

She didn't look great. Her skin was pale, and she had dark shadows under her eyes.

"Don't lie to me," he said. "Didn't you sleep well?"

She gave him a challenging look, as if she was about to tell him not to boss her about, but in the end, she just said, "Not really. Part of the brain injury, apparently. I dozed, but I kept having these vivid dreams…" Her gaze slid past him, as if she was picturing the images in her mind.

"What about?"

"Flashes of light. Screaming. It might be from the accident, even though I can't remember it when I wake up."

"I'm sorry." He dropped to his haunches before her and took her hand in his.

"Going to propose again?" she whispered.

He smiled and brushed his thumb across the back of her hand. "Thank you for coming home with me."

She gave a little shrug. "I thought about it, and you were right that it seems like the best way to try to remember. If anyone's going to jog my memory, I would think it would be my fiancé." She looked up into his eyes then. "You have to promise me, though, that you won't lie to me. If I ask you a question, I need you to tell me the truth. There's no point me trying to rebuild the memories if I'm being given false information."

Rafe was tempted to cross his fingers behind his back, but he just nodded and said, "Of course."

Mollified, she rose and put on her slippers. "Shall we go and have a coffee? Apparently, the doctor won't be around until ten."

"Okay."

They went down to the cafe, and Rafe bought them both a latte and a muffin, under Phoebe's instructions.

"Please tell me I still like muffins," she said as she cut into the chocolate bun.

"Honestly?" He broke open his own. "You don't eat sweet things much either. I can't remember the last time I saw you buy a bar of chocolate."

"Jesus. Are you sure I haven't been possessed? Or taken over by aliens?" She shook her head and had a bite of the muffin. "Seriously, though. It's so weird. I love muffins. And chocolate. And meat! How could I have changed so much and not remember it?"

"I don't know. It is odd, looking back, because you have changed a lot even since I've known you. But of course, it's been gradual for me."

"What was I like when you met me?" She picked a chunk of chocolate off the top of the muffin and popped it into her mouth.

"Like this," he said softly. "Warm. Funny. Feisty."

She frowned and lowered the muffin, staring at it thoughtfully. "So, what am I like now?"

"You're more serious. You work very hard. You're less frivolous."

"I don't sound like a lot of fun."

"Life isn't always about fun," he said. They were her words, although she wouldn't remember saying them. He watched her frown deepen.

"I suppose…" she said slowly.

"We can't stay kids forever," he continued. "We have to grow up sometime." Again, they were her words, and they felt hard and cold in his mouth, like marbles rolling around.

She'd asked him to be honest with her, and he wanted to. He wanted to say that she had become less fun, and that things had been tricky between them because of it. But it wouldn't be fair when she couldn't remember being like that.

She cleared her throat. "All right. I tried to flick through some current events on the iPad—and by the way, oh my God the internet is so fast now! So much better than it was. But anyway, I was too tired to make sense of it all, so I thought I'd leave it to you to educate me."

Leaning back in his chair, he turned his coffee cup in his fingers. "I'm happy to teach you everything I know."

He hadn't meant that to sound sexual, but for some reason it reminded him of when they'd met, and the first few times they'd gone to bed. She hadn't been a virgin, but she hadn't had much experience either, her two previous relationships being short and uninspired. With a propensity to direct in the bedroom, and an enjoyment of trying different positions and places in the house while they made love, he'd introduced her to a wide array of delights, and they'd spent a blissful week where they'd barely gotten out of bed.

"I didn't mean sex," Phoebe said.

He grinned. "Am I that obvious?"

"Your eyes have glazed over."

"You'll have to get used to that."

She gave him a wry look. "I'm not ready for that conversation yet. I meant politics and world events."

"Fair enough." He looked forward to that conversation, though.

He talked for a while about things that had changed since 2010, covering what he thought were the most important events of the decade.

"I was hoping for more general information than who won the rugby world cups," she said after a while.

"Hey, Dan Carter and Richie McCaw's retirement is the biggest thing to happen in New Zealand," he informed her.

"Tell me about the Christchurch earthquakes," she said, leaning her head on a hand.

His smile faded. "One was in September 2010, and then another bigger one followed in February 2011. 185 people were killed in the second one, and it devastated the city. The cathedral was hit and so were half the buildings in the business district. The roads buckled, and homes were broken apart."

"It must have been awful."

"It was shocking. The country's still reeling seven years later."

She clutched her coffee cup, the shadows under her eyes making them seem huge in her skull. "I feel panicky every time I think about the volume of things I don't know. How am I going to function in this world when I can't remember my job or half the people around me?"

"People will make allowances."

"My close friends and family might, but I'm going to look like seven kinds of idiot when I say things that don't make any sense."

"That's how most of us go through life, Phoebe. You need to relax. For the first time in your life, you're out of control, and I know you find it scary, but you're resourceful and smart, and whatever happens to your memory, we'll find a way through. If worst comes to worst, we'll hop on a boat and spend our lives floating around the Pacific Islands or something."

She didn't say anything, and his stomach clenched. She didn't remember him. It was as if a strange guy had walked up to her on the street and suggested she go away with him.

"One step at a time," he suggested.

"Yeah." She finished off her coffee.

"Why don't we go back to your room for a bit? You look tired."

She nodded, and they left the cafe and started walking back along the corridor. At one point, she stumbled, and he slipped an arm around her, holding her tightly while they waited for the elevator. She didn't complain, but she stood stiffly, refusing to relax against him.

When they reached her room, she climbed back onto the bed and curled up on her side.

"Are you staying?" she asked.

"Of course." He sat back in the chair under the window. "I'm not going anywhere."

She closed her eyes, and, within seconds, she was asleep.

Rafe slid down in the seat, leaning his head on the back. She looked frail, much too thin. He'd enjoyed watching her eat the muffin, the sheer way she'd tucked into it. It had been a long time since she'd eaten like that. She picked at her food nowadays like a sparrow, refusing anything except what she needed to fuel her body for her training.

How strange that she didn't remember running. It had become a big part of both of their lives. He hadn't minded; he'd helped with her training, taken her to the events, and had always been supportive, because that's what you did when your partner was passionate about something. He'd stopped at joining her, because he had no interest in spending his free time working so hard, although sometimes they went to the gym together. His job was a physical one, and it was important to keep fit, but it wasn't an obsession for him.

What would happen if her memory didn't return? Would she go back to running? Would it be as if those eight years hadn't happened, and she'd return to being the person she'd been at eighteen? Or would she do something entirely different? None of it was certain. The accident was going to change both their lives in one way or another.

The sun rose in the sky, and Rafe watched her sleep, trying to believe that she wasn't slipping away from him.

Chapter Seven

By eleven-thirty, Phoebe had been cleared by the doctor, and they were in the car, on the road home.

"You're sure about this?" Rafe said. "You don't want one more night there to be on the safe side?"

The doctor had examined her and declared she could go home if she wanted, although he was a little worried about her headaches and the non-return of her memory. But the last thing she needed was to spend another night in the hospital. It was too hot, and the bed was uncomfortable, and even though she'd been lucky enough to have her own room, it was still noisy in the ward, and she'd slept badly.

"No, I'm looking forward to going... home." Her pause was brief, but Rafe glanced at her.

"I know you won't remember it, but don't worry. Hopefully seeing your things around the place will make it comfortable for you."

She nodded, looking out of the window. She was going to take this one tiny step at a time.

"Tell me about being a firefighter," she said, as they left the town of Whangarei behind them and the countryside opened out. It was a beautiful sunny day, and the forested hills in the distance were a rich green, the flat-topped volcanoes standing out against the bright blue sky.

"What do you want to know?" he asked.

"How long have you been one?"

"Since I left school at eighteen. There were seven-hundred applications for forty-eight positions, and I was lucky enough to get one. I took a twelve-week training course in Rotorua, worked in Wellington for a while, then luckily got a transfer back up here."

"Are you from the Bay of Islands?"

"Born and bred in Paihia. It's a good part of the world. Sun, sea, surf, and…" He grinned. She just knew he'd been about to say sex. "Great food," he said instead.

She glanced across at him. Today he was wearing tight dark jeans and an All Blacks short-sleeved rugby shirt. Made of some stretchy material, it fit tightly across his arms and chest. It showed off his defined abs, and… oh my God… was that a six-pack?

"You work out," she stated before she could think better of it.

"I have to stay fit." He glanced at her, and she saw his eyes slide down to her breasts before returning to the road.

"Did you just eye-dip me?" she demanded.

He gave a short laugh. "You were looking at my abs."

"I was doing research."

"Yeah, right," he scoffed. She stuck her tongue out at him, and he laughed.

"It's weird," she said. "You've seen me naked." Of course, she'd seen him naked, too. She'd tugged this guy's shirt up, stripped it off, and run her hands over his smooth, tanned, muscled body. She'd slid down the zipper of his jeans and pulled them off. Then she'd helped him off with his boxers, and… holy moly.

He chuckled. "You've gone scarlet. What are you thinking about?"

"Chocolate," she said.

"Ha! It's good to know you haven't changed that much."

"Rafe! Jeez. Let's change the subject."

"What do you want to talk about?"

"Tell me about our social life. Our friends. What do we do in our spare time?"

"I'll tell you," he said, "but of course we're moving soon, so everything's going to change."

He started to talk about their friends and the places they went for a drink in the evenings, but Phoebe couldn't help but ponder on what he'd said. There was definitely an undercurrent beneath his words. A friction between them concerning the move to Auckland.

Thinking too hard made her brain hurt, though, so she filed it away for later, and listened to him talk about their friends. Most of the names he mentioned she didn't know, people he obviously worked with and their partners, friends she'd made along the way.

"I'm going to have to meet everyone at some point," she said. "That's going to be so embarrassing when I don't remember their names."

"You've had a brain injury. Everyone's just thrilled you're alive. And don't worry. We'll take it easy the first few days. I'm not going to drag you around to see everyone. I want this time to be about you and me."

She looked out of the window, not sure how to reply. Maybe she should have stayed with her mother after all. The thought of being the focus of Rafe's attention made goosebumps rise on her skin. What on earth was she doing? How could she have thought this was a good idea?

"You look worried," he said. "What's on your mind?"

"I'm thinking about the wedding," she replied. "A lot of organization must have gone into it. If we wait too long to cancel, it'll be a waste of a lot of money. Wouldn't it be best to do it sooner rather than later?"

"For a start, we're not exactly getting married at Westminster Abbey. We both decided on a very quiet, small affair, fifty guests, minimum fuss. We're not planning D-Day. And secondly, it's not an issue. We won't be cancelling." His voice held the hint of steel she was beginning to recognize.

She glanced across at him. "You're serious about wanting it to go ahead still, aren't you?"

"Dead serious. I've waited long enough to put a ring on your finger. I'm not letting a little thing like you forgetting my name delay it." He gave a small smile, but she could see he meant what he said. He really expected her to stand beside him at the altar in ten days' time and say 'I do.' He was either delusional or supremely confident of his ability to charm her. She felt a twinge of irritation at the knowledge that it was likely to be the latter.

Well, she wasn't going to fall at his feet just because he had a twinkle in his eye, the cocky bastard. He was very nice, and she suspected that when she got her mojo back she'd be getting all the feels physically, but at that moment, if her memory didn't return, she couldn't imagine any way she would be marrying him.

Marriage wasn't something to be entered into lightheartedly. All relationships involved a certain amount of power play, and she felt uneasy that she couldn't remember what theirs was like. Several times, she'd had the feeling he was hiding something from her. Marrying him without remembering would involve a large degree of trust that she'd been happy and knew what she was doing. But right at that moment, she didn't trust anyone, including herself. She wasn't going to marry him just because she was worried about upsetting him, or disappointing her family, or cancelling the flowers. She would marry a man only because she loved him and wanted to spend the rest of her life with him, and at that moment, she didn't feel that way about Rafe.

Besides which, where was the harm in delaying the wedding for a few months? What was the hurry?

"Give me a week," he said as if he'd read her mind. "Next Saturday, we'll sit down and have a serious talk about what we're going to do, and it'll still give us three days to cancel, if that's really what you want. Until then, try not to stress about it. We just need to spend some time together and get to know each other again. I know you don't remember me, but in an odd way you're a stranger to me, too."

She frowned, puzzled. "Have I changed so much over the past few years?"

"Well, yes. I don't mean to belittle what you're going through, but this isn't easy for me either. You're not the woman I was going to marry. And yet you are, of course. I can't quite square it in my head."

She hadn't thought of it like that. It must be very difficult for him, not just because she didn't remember him, but because she seemed to have changed so much. She felt a twinge of pity for him. "That's fair enough. I promise I'll give it a few days and I won't rush the decision."

"I can't ask more than that." He glanced at her. "Why don't you close your eyes for a bit?"

"I'm not tired." But she was, of course, and even before he answered, she let her eyelids drift shut.

"I'll be here," he said softly. "I'll look after you."

I know, she wanted to answer, but tiredness had overtaken her, and she drifted away.

*

When she woke again, they'd taken the turnoff from the state highway to Kerikeri, and were heading into town.

"I slept the whole way," she said in dismay, straightening in the seat. "I'm so sorry."

"You're going to need to rest a lot," Rafe said, glancing over at her. "Don't worry about it."

She looked down as he squeezed her fingers. He'd been holding her hand. As she watched, he withdrew his and returned it to the wheel.

Not saying anything, she turned her attention to the town as he drove through it.

"It doesn't look much different," she said. "Some new shops. Some I remember."

"There's the Bay of Islands Brides." Rafe slowed the car and pointed to a shop on her left. Phoebe caught her breath at the sight of the large shop window with its display of beautiful gowns, and the Bridal Cafe next to it, with chairs and tables spilling onto the sunlit path. "I can stop if you want," he said.

"No, maybe tomorrow." One step at a time, she reminded herself.

"Okay." He drove through the town and over the bypass, then back down toward the river, finally turning onto a side road, then pulling onto a drive fronting a long, low house. "Home," he said, turning off the engine and smiling.

Phoebe got out of the car, her heart picking up speed at the thought that this was the home she shared with Rafe. This was where they were going to live as a married couple. A row of smallish pohutukawa trees hid the house from the road, and it seemed to nestle in the surrounding bush. The front lawn was carefully tended, scattered with lilac-colored petals from the large jacaranda tree in the middle. The wooden walls were painted a rich cream that made it glow in the afternoon sun.

Rafe collected her bag from the car, then took her hand and led her toward the front door. He unlocked it and stood back to let her through.

She slipped past him into the cool interior, and found herself in a large open-plan room, with a kitchen to her left and a living room in front of her. The whole front wall was glass, and it overlooked a deck, and from that a bank leading down to the inlet.

Rafe took her bag along a corridor to her left behind the kitchen, presumably to one of the bedrooms. She stepped down into the living room and walked slowly across it. There were signs of a female presence around, which must mean they were her things—a pair of feminine slippers under the table, half a dozen bridal magazines on its surface, a calendar on the wall covered with handwriting that she recognized as her own listing people's birthdays and anniversaries. A box with a big label saying 'Wedding' in fancy script rested on a desk in the corner. Above it, another calendar on the wall bore a countdown to their wedding. She opened the box to find a neat pile of folders labelled with things like 'Flowers' and 'Catering'. Each of them held flyers, a list of phone numbers, photographs cut from magazines, and a timeline of the organization she'd done.

She closed the box and glanced over her shoulder at Rafe. He stood in the center of the room, his hands in the pockets of his jeans.

"What do you think?" he asked.

"It's nice." She turned slowly, looking at the artwork on the walls, the cushions on the sofa and chairs. Had she chosen the decor? Had she bought that ornament, knitted that sweater slung over the chair? "I don't remember it, though," she whispered, turning back to him. "I'm sorry."

"It's okay."

Tears filled her eyes. "I really thought it would jog my memory, and everything would come rushing back."

"Hey." He walked up to her, taking his hands out of his pockets. "It's all right. It's just going to take time."

But the tears spilled over her lashes, and she couldn't stop them.

"Come here," he said, and, without asking, he pulled her into his arms and hugged her tightly.

She stood there stiffly for a moment, her heart hammering at what felt like an invasion of her space, but he didn't let her go, and eventually she forced herself to relax. Turning her head to rest her cheek on his shoulder, she closed her eyes and inhaled. He'd used a body wash that smelled of lime and mint. His young, strong body felt warm and hard against her fingers as she splayed a hand on his chest.

He rubbed her back and murmured softly in her ear, words meant to console, "There, there," and, "It'll be okay."

"I want to remember," she said. "I want my life back."

"I know."

"I miss it, even though I don't remember it. Does that make sense?"

"Sort of."

I miss you, she thought, although she didn't say it. Being this close to him felt a strange mixture of weird and familiar. In her head, she was eighteen, untouched, her only experience with love a brief relationship with a guy at sixteen that hadn't developed into anything more intimate than kissing in the trees around the school fields. How strange was that? Rafe had suggested that they'd set the bed alight, but although she understood the mechanics, she didn't remember how to please a man. If she were to go to bed with him, he'd be disappointed that she didn't know what to do.

She pushed back a little, and wiped her face. "Could I have a drink?"

He dropped his arms. "Of course. Why don't you sit on the sofa, and I'll make us a coffee. Maybe we'll watch a movie? Would you like that?"

She nodded and walked over to the TV as he went into the kitchen. "This screen's huge."

"We're big fans of watching TV. It's our one real vice."

"Where are the DVDs?"

He started making the coffee. "We got rid of them all. Everything's online now. Have a look at Netflix."

She turned on the TV, startled to find it like a big phone, with apps on the screen she could highlight and choose. Bringing up Netflix, she stared in wonder at all the series and movies available. "Wow. What shall we watch?" She scrolled through the movies. "What was the first movie we saw together?"

"We saw something called *Pride and Prejudice and Zombies*."

"Seriously?"

He laughed. "Yeah, I know it doesn't sound like a first date movie, but it was brilliant. You loved it. Go to Google Play—we own it on there."

She followed his directions and brought it up. "Can we watch it now?"

"Sure." He brought their drinks over to the coffee table and sat beside her on the sofa. She pressed play, and they settled back to watch the movie. He sat with one arm stretched out along the back of the sofa, almost around her, but not quite, his thigh a few inches from hers. He still smelled gorgeous. Part of her wanted to snuggle up to him, not for any sexy reason, just to be close to him, because she realized he made her feel safe. The photos on her phone had proven that they were a couple, and the way he acted told her how he felt about her.

She wasn't ready to return to being lovers. But he was hers, and she was his, and she didn't mind that as much as she had at the beginning.

Chapter Eight

After a few minutes, Rafe's phone buzzed in his pocket, and he slid it out to check the message.

"Am I stopping you from doing something?" Phoebe asked.

"No, of course not." He tapped a quick message in, sent it, and tossed the phone aside. "That was Josh, asking how you are. People have been asking continually. Everyone's concerned."

"I don't want to see anyone yet," she said in a small voice.

"I know. I'll deal with them."

Phoebe leaned her head on the back of the sofa, her eyes meeting his. He longed to reach out and caress her hair, but he was worried about touching a sore spot, and besides, he didn't think she would want him to. He understood, but it made him sad that she was being so reticent. Maybe he'd been wrong in trying to push for the wedding to go ahead. Perhaps he should have acted as if he'd never met her either, then of course they wouldn't be getting married in ten days.

She was still studying him, a puzzled look on her face.

"What?" he asked softly.

"Why me?"

"What do you mean?"

"Why did you choose me?" She looked genuinely bewildered. "You're gorgeous. Sexy. You could have any woman you want. Why me?"

Warmth spread through him at the thought that she still thought he was sexy. But he just smiled. "Because you were the most beautiful woman I'd ever seen, inside and out."

"Yeah, right," she scoffed, but he didn't look away.

He turned in the seat a little to face her, captivated by her shining green eyes. "When I walked into the bar with Elliot, I saw you right across the room. You were standing talking to some friends. You'd been to a big bridal convention in Auckland with your mum and sisters where you'd been showing some of your dresses. You were wearing a pale pink pantsuit with a white blouse and high heels—you stood out amongst the women in the bar, so elegant, full of confidence. Elliot saw me staring and laughed, and took me right up to you and introduced us. We went over to a table and sat for an hour, just talking. You were the nicest person I'd ever met, gentle, kind. And funny, you made me laugh all the time. I fell in love with you right away."

A flush filled her cheeks. "You're just saying that."

"Nope. I rang you a couple of days later and asked you to come to the movies with me, and you said yes. I put my arm around you as soon as we sat down, and you laughed and said, 'You don't waste much time,' but you didn't push me away, and I was over the moon. I walked you home, and I kissed you that night. I had stars in my eyes."

It gave him a glow inside to remember those early days. He still loved her deeply, but there was no doubt that life had taken its toll on their relationship. It was still as passionate as it had been back then, more so maybe, as they knew each other well and were extremely compatible in the bedroom. But the pressures and frustrations of daily life had molded and changed them, and the last few months, especially, had been trying.

But Phoebe didn't remember any of that. She was looking at him the way she had that evening in the bar. *You're gorgeous. Sexy.* It sent a tingle through him that started at his toes and went all the way up to the roots of his hair.

"It's odd," she whispered, "I keep forgetting we're engaged. And then I remember, and I think well, it's okay if I have feelings for you— I'm supposed to! I could hug you or kiss you and I wouldn't be forward or tarty; in fact it's good that I feel that way. But then I think of actually doing it, and I go all hot inside."

He chuckled. "Just go with the flow."

She nibbled her bottom lip, her gaze flicking to his arm, but she still didn't say anything.

"Want a hug?" he said.

Her eyes came back to his, and she gave a little nod.

He moved his arm around her shoulders, and she curled up against him.

Rafe gave a silent sigh and pressed his lips to her hair. Maybe there was hope that this was going to work out after all.

"You smell good," she said.

"Why, thank you."

"I must smell awful. I need a shower."

"Well, you don't, so let's tackle that tomorrow. Just rest, today."

She nodded and laid her head on his shoulder.

Ten minutes later, Rafe felt her growing heavy against him, and he looked down at her face to see her eyes closed. Turning a little on the sofa, he stretched out his legs and lay back, tucking a cushion under his head, and bringing Phoebe with him. Without waking, she nestled up to him, and he tightened his arms around her.

He left the movie on, half watching it as he dozed himself, content to just lie there with her in his arms.

*

When she awoke, it was nearly five p.m. The movie had finished, and Rafe was getting stiff, but he hadn't wanted to disturb her.

"Jesus," she said, pushing on his chest to lift herself up. "I'm so sorry."

"It's okay." He rose too, stood, and stretched. "How are you feeling?"

"Hungry. And I have a headache."

"It's time for your painkillers. Come on, I'll start some dinner."

He led her up to the kitchen and poured her a glass of water, and she took her medication while he opened the fridge and investigated the contents. "What do you fancy tonight?"

She picked up a pack of two sirloin steaks he'd bought for himself.

His eyebrows rose. "Seriously?"

She shrugged. "Might as well before I go back to being all self-righteous."

"Whatever the lady wants. I'll do a blue cheese sauce, how about that?"

"Sounds lovely. Um… I thought I might change?"

"Sure." He led the way down the corridor. "This is our bedroom." He took her into the large room with the floor-to-ceiling windows that overlooked the river. "You can sleep here tonight; I'll take the sofa."

"Don't we have a spare room?"

"Yeah, but we've got a lot of fitness equipment in there. The sofa's comfy enough."

Turning away, he pulled open the chest of drawers nearest the window. "This one's yours. And your clothes are hanging up there."

He indicated the wardrobe on the right. She opened it and ran a hand across the skirts, suits, and dresses.

He opened his own drawers and took out a clean tee and a pair of shorts. Without thinking, he tugged his All Blacks shirt over his head and tossed it onto the bed, then went to unbutton his jeans. He stopped as he realized she was staring at him, her gaze sliding to the muscles on his chest.

"Oops," he said. "Sorry. It was automatic." Grabbing the items, he went into the *en suite* bathroom behind them, sprayed on some deodorant, then changed his clothes, only emerging when he was fully dressed.

Phoebe's gaze raked him, and he wasn't sure if it was relief or disappointment in her eyes when she saw him clothed.

"I thought I might put a nightie or some PJs on, just to be comfortable," she said.

"Ah… I don't think you own any. You don't wear anything in bed."

Her eyebrows rose. "Oh." Her face went scarlet.

He tried not to laugh. "Your T-shirts are in that drawer. I'll be in the kitchen."

He left her to it, chuckling to himself, and started on the steak, rubbing some spices into the meat before heating up the oil.

She came out a few minutes later. To his surprise, she was wearing one of his tees over a pair of track pants. "Hope you don't mind," she said, taking a seat on one of the stools by the breakfast bar. "It's nice and loose."

"Of course not. It looks better on you."

"It smells nice too." She lifted it and buried her nose in it.

He turned away to fetch some herbs from the fridge, hiding a smile.

"Dinner's nearly ready," he said. "I thought we could finish off the potato salad I bought yesterday on the way home, and have it with a green salad. Okay?"

"Sounds lovely."

He dished the steaks up, poured over a little of the blue cheese sauce he'd made, and took the plates outside to the table on the deck, putting up the umbrella to shade them from the sun.

"Better not have wine," he said, bringing out two glasses of iced water.

"Please tell me I haven't given up alcohol," she said, taking a seat.

"No, you still like a glass of Sauvignon." He took the seat opposite her, watching as she cut into the steak.

"Glad to hear it." She ate a mouthful, her eyes closing in blissful appreciation. "Oh, that's amazing. It's so tender. Do you do most of the cooking?"

"Nah, we tend to share. We've actually been to a couple of cooking classes together."

"Oh? Really?"

"Yeah, they were fun. Run by a chef up in Mangonui. The dessert class was very… entertaining." His gaze slid to the distance as he remembered making profiteroles at home with her. He'd deliberately left some whipped cream in the bowl, and he'd taken great delight in spreading it over her and licking it all off later on.

He moved his gaze back to her. She was watching him, and clearly knew perfectly well what he was thinking.

Smirking, he cut up his steak.

"I'm going to have trouble with you, aren't I?" she said.

"*Moi?*"

"Mum warned me you were irreverent and mischievous."

He chuckled. "Doesn't sound like me at all."

"You have a naughty glint in your eye. I get the feeling you're thinking about me naked more often than not."

"Possibly. I can take my clothes off if you like, then you'll be able to picture me naked whenever you want."

"That won't be necessary."

"Are you sure? I saw the way you looked at me in the bedroom." Her eyes had nearly come out on stalks when he'd stripped off his T-shirt.

"I did not!"

He just grinned and ate a mouthful of potato salad. "You are allowed to look," he pointed out. "We are engaged."

"Jesus."

"You can touch too, if you like. Wanna feel my biceps?"

"Stop it," she scolded with some exasperation.

He laughed and gestured at her plate. "Are you enjoying that steak?" There was hardly any of it left.

"It's amazing. I'm still not sure I'm vegetarian. I think you were lying to me when you told me that."

"No, I wasn't." But he couldn't stop a little twinge of guilt inside at the thought that he had lied to her. Or, at least, he'd omitted to tell the truth. Noelle might have instigated it, but he was perpetuating the lie by not being completely honest with her.

He wasn't going to worry about it now, though. Not when he had Phoebe there, in the house. There was plenty of time to introduce her to the details of their past. First, he had to win her back, and then maybe, when he did reveal everything, it wouldn't mean the end of their relationship.

Clearing his throat, he changed the subject, asking her what she'd like to watch on TV after they'd eaten. They talked about movies while they finished their dinner, and then the phone rang, and it was Noelle wanting to see how her daughter was getting on. So Rafe left them to talk while he cleaned up the dinner things and stacked the dishwasher. He could hear Phoebe talking, though, out on the deck, and he heard her defending him, saying, "He's being great, Mum. He's really looking after me, don't worry."

When she eventually came in, he was sitting on the sofa, flicking through the movies on the TV.

"Everything all right?" he asked.

"She's just worried." She sat next to him. "It's odd, but even though I don't remember the last eight years, I know I'm not eighteen. Does that make sense? I don't want to go home and be fussed over by my mother. I love her, but somehow I know that's not my place anymore."

"Where is your place?" he asked.

She met his gaze, her green eyes shining. "I'm not saying I'm ready to slip back to the way we were."

"I know."

"But I can tell you care for me. I know I belong here. I just… need time, that's all."

"I know." He stretched his legs out on the coffee table and raised his arm.

She looked at it for a moment, and then her lips curved up, and she moved closer to him on the sofa. He lowered his arm around her. He couldn't help but notice the way her breasts moved beneath the T-shirt fabric; she'd taken off her bra. His body stirred, but he quashed his desire impatiently. He might be used to them having sex all the time, but he was a grown man—he could manage a few weeks without it for Christ's sake!

It wasn't easy when she was leaning against him, though, all soft in his arms. His body wanted her, even though his mind scolded it for thinking about sex when she wasn't well. The last time they'd made love had been on this very sofa, with her sitting astride him. It was impossible to rid himself of the images of her naked, of closing his mouth over her nipples, of her tipping back her head as she cried out with passion.

He shifted on the sofa, trying not to get a hard-on. That was the last thing she needed to see.

They chose a movie, and this time she stayed awake through it. It felt like old times, watching cuddled up, discussing what the actors had been in before, talking about the plot points and their favorite bits. It ended too soon for Rafe, but even though it was only eight thirty, Phoebe was yawning, and he knew it was time for her to go to bed.

"Come on, sleepy." He stopped and pulled her to her feet, and led her through to the bedroom. "Go and clean your teeth, and I'll get the bed ready."

She went into the bathroom and closed the door, and he pulled back the duvet for her, closed the curtains, turned on the bedside light, and fetched her a glass of water. She came out, and he held the duvet up while she slid beneath it.

She sat up, her arms around her knees, watching him as he retrieved her medication and handed it to her. She took it mutely, swallowing it down with the water. Her face was pale, and the dark shadows were back under her eyes.

"Is your head bad?" he asked.

"It's throbbing, yeah. It's making me feel a bit queasy."

"I hope that wasn't the steak. Your stomach isn't used to meat."

"I'm sure I'll be fine." She didn't look fine, though.

He hesitated. "I'll only be in the living room. If you call out, I'll hear you."

She nodded, but her eyes glistened; she wasn't far from tears. "I feel a bit sorry for myself, that's all," she whispered, touching her hand to the back of her head.

"I'm not surprised." An idea came to him, and he smiled. "I'll be back in a minute."

He went into the living room, closed all the windows, locked the doors, and turned off the lights. Then he went into the spare room, where the rowing machine and weights were. In the corner was a mattress he'd used a couple of times when friends had come over to stay. He brought it and the spare duvet back with him into the main bedroom.

"I'll sleep here," he told her, laying it beside the bed. "That way I'll be here if you need me."

Phoebe's bottom lip trembled. "You don't have to do that."

"Sweetheart, I'd do anything for you. Now lie down and go to sleep. You need to get a good night's rest, and then tomorrow we can start going to a few places to see if we can jog your memory."

He went to the bathroom and cleaned his teeth, then came out and turned off the main light. He stretched out on the mattress, plumping the pillows behind his head, pulled the duvet over him, and lay down.

He picked up his book and opened it to where he'd left the bookmark. Then he glanced up. Phoebe was looking down at him, resting her cheek on her hand. Without saying anything, she lowered her other hand. He clasped it in his, lifted his head, and kissed her fingers. Then he lay back and started reading his book.

Chapter Nine

"So, what would you like to do today?"

Phoebe crunched her toast, studying Rafe as she considered his question. The guy had an inherent sexiness that filtered into everything he did. Did he have any idea how gorgeous he looked at that moment, sitting at the breakfast bar in a faded tee and scruffy shorts and bare feet, his hair all mussed and a day's growth of beard on his jaw? His blue eyes were half-lidded in the way that she'd thought meant he was thinking about sex, but that couldn't be true, because they were like that most of the day. He couldn't be thinking about sex all the time.

She moved to get her glass of orange juice, and his gaze dropped to where the T-shirt stretched over her breasts. He *was* thinking about sex. Jesus. The man was insatiable.

His gaze came back to hers, and she arched an eyebrow. He just gave her an impish smile.

She couldn't bring herself to berate him, though. She was incredibly touched by how he'd lain by the bed all night, and had woken immediately whenever she'd roused. At one point, she'd jerked awake from a violent dream of broken glass and flashing lights, her head throbbing, to find him sitting on the side of the bed, holding her hand. He'd given her some more painkillers, and had then refused to move until she'd dozed off again. He really seemed to care about her.

Crunching her toast again, she gave him a small smile.

"So," he said. "Plans?"

She hesitated. "I don't know. What do you think?"

"I guess it depends on how you're feeling. You still look tired."

"I feel tired. And… I don't know. A bit… confused, I suppose. Like my brain's working super slowly. It feels rubbery, like it's rebelling when I try to think."

"We shouldn't push you too hard."

"No, I suppose not. Although… I do want to remember. I thought… Maybe we should go to the shop."

Rafe pushed away his empty plate and leaned back. "Are you sure you're ready for that?"

"I don't know, maybe not. But after you, I thought the shop would be one of the places that might jog my memory."

"Okay. I'll ring Noelle and tell her we'll be down mid-morning. Would you like a shower today?"

"I'd love one. And I really need to wash my hair, although I've got to be careful of the dressing, obviously."

"I can get in the shower with you if you like."

She shivered at the thought of him naked and slippery, pressed up against her. "Thank you, Rafe. I don't think that's a good idea."

He grinned. "I can help you wash your hair over the sink if you want."

"That might be a better idea."

"Come on, then."

He led her into the bathroom, ran the sink full of warm water, and retrieved a plastic jug from the kitchen. She leaned over the sink and closed her eyes, feeling his hands in her hair, wetting it while carefully avoiding the wound. Then he poured a little shampoo into his hands, and she felt him massage it into her hair, his fingers gentle against the left side of her scalp. It was an innocent touch, not at all sexual, and yet there was something so sensual about it that she almost groaned out loud.

He rinsed it with water from the jug, squeezed the excess water from the ends, and placed a towel over it, massaging it slowly.

"Thank you," she said from beneath the towel.

"You're welcome." His voice was a little husky. Had it affected him, too?

She lifted her head, and found herself looking up into his eyes. He slid a hand beneath her chin, and for a moment she thought he was going to kiss her. She wanted him to. It didn't matter that she couldn't remember their time together, something deep inside her still felt that connection with him.

Or was she just being fanciful? He was young, handsome, and sexy; any woman in her position would be getting all the feels, wouldn't she? She mustn't mistake basic desire for something deeper.

To her joint disappointment and relief, he didn't kiss her. He wiped the drips from around her face with the towel, then opened one of the drawers under the sink and retrieved a hair clip.

"Thanks," she said, turning to look into the mirror as she clipped up her hair ready for the shower.

Rafe stood behind her, and then, to her surprise, he slid his arms around her and rested his lips on her shoulder. She was still wearing his T-shirt, but the heat of his body burned against her back, and, in the mirror, she saw her nipples tighten through the fabric. She was sure he'd seen it too—he wouldn't have missed something like that—but he didn't say anything, he just held her, his arms tight around her waist.

"I miss you," he mumbled against her shoulder.

She rested her arms over his. His skin was warm, his tanned arms covered with light brown hair touched with gold from the sun. They were well-muscled arms, and his hands were large and strong. She could imagine them sliding over her pale skin, touching, stroking…

"I'm still here," she whispered, but she knew what he meant. He missed the intimacy of their previous relationship, kissing her, making love to her.

He didn't move for a moment, and she closed her eyes, the sun warming her as it slanted through the bathroom window, and Rafe heating her up from the inside just by being so close to her. She was healing physically—she could feel it, the wound closing together, the damaged skin shedding, cells renewing. It would take time until she was back to normal, but she was on the road to recovery.

But emotionally? Mentally? How could she even begin to heal until she could remember her past?

She opened her eyes, thinking how pale her skin was next to Rafe's. Her eyes still bore dark shadows beneath them, and her skin looked almost translucent. In contrast, he was the picture of health, radiating energy—she could almost feel herself sucking it in, desperately trying to refill her empty well.

"What's the catch?" she asked, watching as he lifted his head to meet her eyes in the mirror.

"What do you mean?"

"You're gorgeous. Sexy. You obviously know your way around the bedroom. You cook. You're smart. You're kind and caring. What's the catch? There must be one."

He kissed her shoulder, then released her and turned to switch on the shower. "Well, thank you for those compliments. But I'm no chef—I can just throw a few bloke's dishes together. I'm caring because you need help at the moment, but you've accused me in the past of being thoughtless and unfeeling."

"Have I?" The thought embarrassed her. "I'm sorry."

He laughed. "I probably was. I have many faults. I'm impatient, selfish, irritable when I don't get what I want… I'm hardly perfect."

She didn't say anything, because she hadn't seen any of those things in him. But then again, she'd only known him a few days. Maybe if she lived with him for six months, he'd irritate her.

Or maybe not.

She watched him test the temperature of the water, and then he turned back to her. "Want me to help you in?" he suggested.

"I'm good, thanks."

He gave an exaggerated sigh. "Okay. I might do a quick workout in the spare room before I have my shower."

"Sure."

She watched him go and shut the door behind him. Her hand rested on the lock. They lived together. They were getting married. Was she being dumb locking the door on him? She felt guilty at feeling uncomfortable, then locked the door crossly and stripped off Rafe's T-shirt. She was going to do what made sense. Screw what she was supposed or not supposed to feel.

She took her time showering, picking up the various body washes on the shelf and sniffing them, wondering if it was she who had bought them a week or two before. Using the mint one, she washed her skin, wincing as the occasional graze stung, then came out and dried herself.

Letting the towel drop, she studied herself in the mirror. Gosh, she was so thin. She must have lost a lot of weight recently with her training. She'd been plump as a teen, and it was nice to be on the thin side, but it was odd to see her hipbones jutting out. Her arm and leg muscles were toned, and her stomach was flat. Her breasts were high and firm.

Rafe had said *You were quite curvy when I met you*. Did he mind that she'd lost her roundness? She wondered whether he resented all the training she did. He hadn't said in so many words, but she couldn't shake the feeling that there was a riptide running beneath their relationship that he was hiding from her, something that was going to pull her under when she least expected it.

Sighing, she wrapped a towel around her body before coming out into the bedroom. Rafe wasn't there, and, in the distance, she could hear a machine going, and it sounded as if he was running. She opened her wardrobe and chose a dark blue dress with colored flowers that appealed to her and slipped it on, then dried her hair, smoothing it carefully over the dressing on the back, and securing it with a simple band so it covered the wound.

The exertion of getting ready had tired her, but she was determined not to be beaten, so she wandered through to the other side of the house to the spare room, and paused in the doorway.

Rafe was on the treadmill, running flat out, rock music leaking from his earbuds. Sweat stained the back of his T-shirt in a dark V both back and front, and his face and neck glistened.

Phoebe leaned against the doorjamb, spellbound. The guy was a wonder to behold. She could see from the weights in the room that he worked out a lot, and he had strong, powerful thighs and muscular arms. He looked at the peak of fitness, and he was gorgeous.

Tired as she was, she felt a stirring deep inside her, a sexual attraction to him that spoke of something deeper and darker than a mere flirtation. This man had coaxed her to the height of pleasure many, many times. Somehow, her body remembered his touch, even if she didn't.

He glanced at the door, did a double take, and his eyebrows rose. A smile spread across his face. Phoebe smiled back, but she didn't move.

He continued running for a few minutes, but he was obviously conscious of her watching him. Eventually, he slowed the machine, then stopped and jumped down.

Picking up a towel, he walked over to her.

"You look good," he said, pausing in front of her.

"You're all sweaty," she pointed out.

He put his hands on his hips. Jeez, the energy this guy was exuding. He could power the whole of Kerikeri with it.

"You like me being sweaty," he said. His eyes were so hot she could feel her insides melting.

She lifted her chin. "That was old Phoebe."

He moved a bit closer to her. The hollow at the base of his throat glistened. "Really," he said.

She was sooooo tempted to lean forward and touch her tongue there. "Really," she told him. "I could smell you from Mars. You're disgusting." It was a lie—he smelled of hot, healthy male, and the word disgusting was at the opposite end of the spectrum to what she felt. The thought of sliding her hands under his damp T-shirt, of scoring her nails up his glowing back, gave her all kinds of tingles.

He gave a small laugh and looked down at himself. "Yeah, fair enough." He stepped closer to her to go through the door.

Phoebe didn't move.

He stopped and looked down at her. He topped her by about six inches, and her heart rate increased as his eyes met hers.

He didn't say anything. Keeping his amused, hot gaze on hers, he squeezed by her, not bothering to breathe in as his chest brushed her arm, then walked off down the corridor to the bathroom, the towel over his shoulder.

Her lips curving up, Phoebe went into the kitchen to pour herself a cold drink.

Chapter Ten

It was the height of summer, and the weather had turned hot and humid. Sitting in the car before Rafe turned on the air conditioning, Phoebe felt sweat trickling between her breasts. As soon as he turned it on, though, cool air flowed over her, and she blew out a breath and relaxed back in the seat.

"You okay?" he asked, heading the car out onto the main road. "You still look pale."

"I'm tired."

"You sure you want to do this now?"

"Yes," she said, although part of her wished she'd just stayed indoors with Rafe, watching movies, and letting him cook for her. "Did you ring Mum?"

"Yes. They're looking forward to seeing you."

Phoebe looked out of the window and didn't reply. Nerves fluttered in her stomach, not so much at the thought of seeing her mother, but at seeing Bianca and Roberta. She hated that Bianca was upset with her for moving away. They'd never been the sort of sisters who bickered or argued over boys and clothes. They'd been each other's best friends all the way through school, and she'd been looking forward to going to university together. To think that there was friction between them… jeez. How had she dealt with that? She must have really loved the idea of working at Mackenzie's if she'd been willing to jeopardize her relationship with her family.

Or maybe Rafe hadn't given her a choice. She had to remember that.

"Hey." He picked up her hand and squeezed her fingers. "Don't worry. It'll be fine."

"Is the job at Mackenzie's really spectacular? I mean, what does it offer me to make me want to leave here?"

He returned his hand to the wheel, navigating the roundabout. "It's a big company, and the shop in Auckland is huge, right in the middle of Queen Street. Lisa Mackenzie has offered you the position of Marketing Director."

"Jesus."

"It's a big step up for you, especially considering you're only twenty-six."

"But… Marketing Director? Does that mean I won't be sewing anymore?"

"You'll be in charge of how the company presents itself to its customers. Of organizing whole collections of gowns."

He was avoiding the question, but she knew she was right.

Marketing Director? What the hell did she know about marketing? What was it they said about promoting to a level of incompetence? Why on earth had she thought she'd enjoy a job like that?

She didn't say anything else as they drove through the town, and Rafe parked opposite the shop.

He got out of the car and shut his door, then stopped as he obviously realized she wasn't getting out. When she didn't move, he walked around to the passenger door, opened it, and leaned on the top as he bent to look at her.

"What's the matter?" he asked softly.

"I don't know if I'm ready for this."

"It's just a shop, Phoebe. You don't have to make any decisions or anything yet. Come on. You'll feel better once you've taken this step." He held out a hand.

Swallowing hard, she took it and let him pull her to her feet, and then lead her across the road.

The door jangled as they entered. The shop was cool, and seemed filled with light and air. Golden bars of sunlight streamed through the high windows to fall across the cream carpet, while a small crystal chandelier in the center filled the room with sparkles of light.

The gowns were hung on long rails that ran down the left wall, with a couple displayed on mannequins at either end. On the far side was a large dressing room filled with mirrors, where a young woman was trying on a dress, turning around to see herself from all sides. Shelves of wedding shoes, tiaras, and other accessories filled part of the wall to the right, but there was also a big opening to the cafe next door, where Phoebe could see half-a-dozen tables and a counter filled with muffins and cakes. The young woman's friends, in the middle of sipping their lattes, squealed with delight as she walked into the middle of the main room to show off her choice of gown, its beading glittering in the light from the chandelier.

"Phoebe!" Noelle came forward to give her daughter a hug. "Oh, it's lovely to see you. How are you feeling?"

"I'm okay. A bit tired, but on the mend, I think."

"Good. You look better."

"I don't, but thank you anyway."

"I was being polite. But you're still beautiful." Noelle kissed her temple. "Come on, have a look around." Noelle led her into the shop and then let her go.

Phoebe walked slowly along the line of wedding dresses, brushing her fingers across the magnificent plastic-coated gowns. She was conscious of her mother and Rafe watching her, but she tried to shut out their breathless anticipation and focus on the quiet beauty of the place.

Her head buzzed. It was as if a movie was playing in the background, a little out of focus, the music too low to make out. The memories were still there; she could see them like ghosts out of the corner of her eye, but they would not come when she called them.

She reached the end of the rail, and stopped in front of a mannequin wearing a glorious dress.

"This is one of ours," Noelle said softly from beside her.

Phoebe reached out a hand and touched the bodice of the dress. Cut with a sweetheart neckline, it had been embroidered with white flowers all along the edge, which had then been outlined with the tiniest silver beads.

"It's exquisite. I did this?"

Noelle nodded. "You're an amazing designer."

Phoebe looked up, about to answer, but her gaze fell on a doorway to the left of the fitting rooms, and the words died on her lips.

"Go on," Noelle said.

Phoebe walked across the carpet to the door, opened it, and stepped inside.

It was the workroom Rafe had mentioned, where she and Bianca worked. And indeed, there was Bianca, standing at a large table covered with a roll of cream satin, cutting carefully around a pattern she'd pinned to the fabric.

Like in the shop, sun streamed through the high windows at the back, filling the room with light. Bianca had the radio on, and she was singing as she worked. The room felt happy. Phoebe looked to the left and saw another table with a comfortable chair, and shelves filled with numerous trays of beads of different sizes and colors. She didn't remember sitting there, but she knew that was where she worked.

Or had worked, at least. She was leaving all this for Auckland, for city life, which she'd always hated. It must have taken them years to get the shop looking like it did. They must have all invested so much time and energy. And she was walking away from it.

To her shock, tears filled her eyes.

Bianca looked up at that moment and saw her. Her face lit with a smile, which faded rapidly as Phoebe's bottom lip trembled.

"Hey." She put down her scissors and came over, as Noelle and Rafe also spotted her rising emotion.

"Sorry." Phoebe sat heavily on a chair that Rafe pulled out for her. She took a couple of deep breaths, trying to calm her hammering heart.

"It's okay. Are you feeling ill?" Bianca tucked a strand of her sister's hair behind her ear, a gesture that made tears tumble over Phoebe's lashes at the thought that they had recently argued.

"Aw, sweetheart." Noelle dropped to her knees and put her arms around her.

Phoebe covered her face with her hands, fighting for control.

"She's very tired," Rafe said from behind her, and she felt him slip a hand onto the nape of her neck, under her hair. He brushed the skin there with his thumb, making her shiver. She was filled with all these conflicting emotions and could make sense of none of them. Why was this so hard?

She wiped her cheeks and bit her trembling lip as she looked at her twin. "Rafe said that we quarreled. I'm so sorry."

Bianca exchanged a glance with their mother and Rafe, her brow furrowing. "Don't worry about that now," she said.

"But it upset you. You don't want me to go. And I hate the thought that we aren't friends anymore."

Bianca's face crumpled, and she threw her arms around her sister. "Of *course* we're still friends. Born together, friends forever, remember?"

Phoebe buried her face in Bianca's shoulder and hugged her tightly. "I don't know why I made the decision to leave the shop. I wish I could remember so I could understand."

"Don't worry about it now," Bianca whispered. "You just have to concentrate on getting better. Once your memory's back, we can all talk about it and decide what to do."

"*If* it comes back. I don't know what I'm going to do if it doesn't." Her head was starting to pound.

"Come on," Rafe said firmly. "One step at a time. There's no point in stressing when you can't do anything about it."

Bianca moved back. "Rafe's right."

"There's plenty of time to sort everything out," Noelle said. "It was lovely of you to call in, but you look very tired. Why don't you let Rafe take you home and have a rest now?"

Phoebe nodded, sniffing, and wiping her face. Rafe held out a hand, and she let him pull her to her feet. Giving a last, long look at the workroom, she followed him out, back into the shop.

"Is Roberta here?" she asked.

"No, it's her afternoon off," Noelle advised. "Libby's covering her today."

Rafe led her through into the cafe. The cream walls bore stencils in the shape of wedding bells around the top, and many of the cakes in the cabinet had a wedding theme, with horseshoes, rings, and hearts drawn in icing. It was a great idea, she thought, a place where brides-to-be could come with their bridesmaids while they tried on dresses, or women with their girlfriends who enjoyed watching others preparing for a wedding.

"Phoebe!" A pretty blonde woman came around the counter as they entered the cafe. She walked up to Phoebe, her face alight with pleasure. "Oh, it's so good to see you."

"Libby!" Phoebe almost laughed as she realized who it was. "Oh my God, you've changed so much!"

Libby looked puzzled, then obviously realized that Phoebe was comparing her to the way she'd been eight years ago. "Oh. Yes, I suppose I have changed a bit."

"A bit?" Libby had possessed teeth that had stuck out and had been all twisted at different angles, had worn her hair in tight pigtails for most of her school life, and she'd been extremely plump. She looked so different! She'd had her teeth done, and now they were completely neat and straight. Her hair was still long, but knotted up in a messy bun. And although she wasn't skinny, she'd lost a good bit of her puppy fat, revealing curves that Phoebe was sure would turn men's heads wherever she went.

"How are you feeling?" Libby asked her.

"Better, but very tired."

"I'm going to take her home now," Rafe said.

Libby nodded. "Well, it was lovely to see you. When you're feeling better, maybe we can catch up over a coffee?"

"Sure," Phoebe said. She turned to kiss her mother and sister goodbye. "I'll call you later?"

"If you feel up to it," Noelle said. She glanced at Rafe, then back at her daughter. "Are you sure you wouldn't rather come home for a while?"

"Rafe's taking very good care of me," she said softly. "Don't worry."

"Just give her time," Noelle said, giving him a warning look. "Don't go trying anything until she's ready."

Phoebe's face warmed. "Oh my God, Mum! I can't believe you just said that."

"I know what he's like," Noelle said. "He can't keep his hands off you."

"I haven't even tried to snog her yet," Rafe said.

Phoebe glanced at him, relieved that he looked amused rather than annoyed. "Let's go," she said, sending her mother a cross look. Noelle just raised her eyebrows, unrepentant.

Waving goodbye to them all, Phoebe followed Rafe out into the sunshine and let the door swing shut behind them.

"I'm so sorry," she said to him as they walked away. "That was embarrassing."

He shrugged. "She's right. I can't keep my hands off you." He gave her a wry smile.

Phoebe held his gaze for a moment, not sure whether he was joking, but he seemed serious.

He studied her for a moment, then took her hand. "Come with me. I want to show you something before we go home."

He led her across the road and up a side alley to a large car park. At the end of the car park, he stopped and gestured to a large building—the cinema.

"That's where we had our first date," he said.

"They rebuilt it," she said, surprised.

"Yes, it has several screens now. Come this way." He led her back through the car park and across the road to the library. A large building in the shape of the bow of a ship, the library stood on the edge of the domain—a huge park. Rafe took her a little way along the edge of the domain to beneath a pohutukawa tree.

He stopped and took her other hand, turning her to face him. "This was where I first kissed you," he said.

Her eyebrows rose. She looked up into his eyes, her heart racing. He was so handsome; just the thought of kissing him made her feel weak at the knees.

I can't keep my hands off you, he'd said.

He glanced down at where they were holding hands, interlinking his fingers with hers. "I'm sad that you don't remember it," he said.

"Perhaps you should kiss me now," she suggested, "see if it jogs my memory?"

He didn't say anything for a moment. Was he wondering if she was serious? Or thinking about what her mother had said, and trying to decide whether he should wait?

The sunlight slanted through the gaps in the leaves, falling on their skin like gold leaf. In the domain, a group of young lads were throwing a rugby ball about; in the children's playground, a toddler squawked, and a couple of others laughed as they chased each other around the swings. Phoebe felt a flutter of happiness, as if a dozen colorful butterflies had danced in the air before her. Was that due to visiting the bridal shop? To feeling better? Or to being here, with Rafe, on this beautiful day?

She'd loved this man so much that she'd wanted to marry him. His sultry eyes were still staring into hers, and suddenly she wanted him to kiss her more than anything in the world.

"Please," she whispered.

His brow furrowed, and then he let go of her hand and lifted his to cup her cheek, brushing her lips with his thumb. He moved a few inches closer to her, sliding his other hand onto her waist. Then he lowered his lips to hers.

She closed her eyes, holding her breath, too nervous to kiss him back. But he didn't seem to mind. His mouth moved across hers slowly as he took his time to kiss her, his lips gentle, and she drifted away into bliss, conscious of the light morning breeze on her limbs, the dappled sun on her face, and the warm smell of sexy male that sent her senses spinning.

Chapter Eleven

Rafe wanted to wrap his arms around Phoebe, plunge his tongue into her mouth, press up against her, and let loose the passion that always rose inside him whenever he was around this gorgeous, sexy girl.

But he made his kisses small and unthreatening, kept his tongue well out of the way, and just enjoyed being close to her at last.

His heart leapt at the thought that she'd asked him to kiss her. Although initially he'd felt confident that he'd be able to win her back again, she'd been so hesitant to let him in, acting as if they were strangers, and he'd had a few flickers of despair that in her new guise she might have changed so much that she didn't find him attractive anymore.

True, she was stiff and unyielding, not pushing him away, but not kissing him back either, but he didn't let that put him off. He'd known her a long time, and felt that he knew her body almost as well as his own. Whenever they'd argued, he'd always been able to tease her out of a bad mood by nuzzling her neck or kissing her, and he put his trust in their past love, hoping that deep within her remained a seed of remembrance that would begin to blossom again when he exposed it to the light.

He pressed his lips to hers as if they had all the time in the world, ignoring the fact that someone across the road at the fire station was probably watching them and would tease him about this later. It was too perfect a day to rush a kiss like this. Phoebe must have used her favorite perfume that morning, because she smelled of summer—of citrus and coconut, and something headier she'd once told him was vetiver when he'd nuzzled her neck and announced she smelled so good he could eat her up—and had promptly done so.

Thinking about going down on her made his head spin, and he exhaled with a tiny growl he hadn't meant, making Phoebe inhale. She lifted her hands to rest on his chest, and for a moment he thought she was going to push him away. But then her fingers clutched at his shirt, and they fanned out, moving over his shoulders and up his neck, into his hair. He shivered as her nails scraped his scalp, and felt her lips curve a little under his. She'd always loved the power she had over him, the way his body seemed to belong to her. Clearly, that hadn't changed.

She softened against him, like a chocolate button left out in the sun, rising on tiptoes and leaning into the kiss. Rafe sighed, wrapping his arms around her. When her lips parted, he didn't waste the opportunity to dip his tongue into her mouth, joy filling him as she returned the thrust shyly, her fingers tightening in his hair.

They exchanged a long, heartfelt, sensual kiss, and when they finally moved back, Rafe felt as if it was Christmas Day and his birthday and Valentine's Day all rolled into one.

"Yowza." Phoebe wiped her mouth with the back of her hand, her eyes wide and a small smile on her lips. "You kiss like a god."

"It helps to have great inspiration." He tucked a strand of her hair behind her ear. His heart continued to race, and he felt a sweep of hope that maybe, just maybe, everything was going to be all right. "Come on, let's get you home. I think you could do with a rest."

He drove her home, and by the time they walked indoors her pale face with the dark shadows under her eyes made him take her straight to the bedroom. He pushed her onto the bed, took off her shoes, and put on the overhead fan. By the time he left the room, her eyes were closed, and she was breathing evenly.

He made himself a cup of coffee and a large sandwich, and took it out onto the deck to eat. Usually he'd have brought his iPad to read, but today he sat in the quiet, thinking about Phoebe.

The fact that Noelle had asked him to keep the truth about her father's death from Phoebe made him feel as if he had spiders under his skin, itching to get out. And, of course, he hadn't yet mentioned the argument they'd had the night before her accident. She deserved to know these things, and it went against the grain to keep them from her.

But maybe Noelle was right. It was very early days, and Phoebe had only just begun to heal. Who knew what the truth would do to her?

He slid down in the chair, leaned his head on the back of the seat, and looked up at the blue sky. He wasn't being one-hundred-percent honest with himself. The fact was that he *liked* Phoebe the way she was at the moment. Although he admired the way she'd thrown herself into her training, and he was proud of her for raising money for charity, he liked that she was more laid back and less intense now. Was that terrible? This was the woman he'd fallen in love with, and the one he'd tried to reach when they'd had that last, awful argument. The guilt and the grief she'd suffered since her father's death had changed her. It had eaten into her, tarnished the shining silver spirit he'd fallen for, and to have her back the way she was, light-hearted and carefree, made his heart sing.

But he would tell her. He couldn't not. He would stick to his plan, and tell her everything a few days before the wedding, once she'd had more time to heal. Hopefully by then, she'd be so in love with him again that it wouldn't matter.

She slept for a couple of hours, and when she woke, her cheeks had a little more color. He made her some lunch, and they sat outside again while she ate it. Afterward, she said she wanted to go for a walk, so he drove them the short distance down to the river, and they walked slowly across the footbridge to Kemp House and the Stone Store, holding hands.

While they watched the geese and ducks on the riverbank, and the teenagers pushing each other off the rocks into the shallow river, Phoebe asked him questions, about places they'd been together, things they'd done, people they knew. Rafe answered them all, painting a picture of their life, hoping he was doing it justice, because they had been happy.

She was quiet afterward, and he squeezed her fingers as they began to walk back, giving her a smile. "You okay?"

"Mmm. Just processing everything."

"Anything seem familiar?"

She shook her head.

"Don't worry," he murmured. "I'm sure it'll come back eventually."

"I don't know." She looked away, down the river to where the fishing boats were heading out toward the bay. "I keep thinking about what I should do if it doesn't. Do I make decisions based on trusting old Phoebe? Or do I make them based on who I am now?"

Rafe said nothing for a moment, not sure how to answer. He knew what he wanted to say, but it wasn't fair to say that. "I would suggest you wait a while. You don't need to make any decisions yet. Hopefully things will become clear for you by the time you have to decide something."

She didn't reply, and he wasn't sure if she was thinking about marrying him or whether the idea of moving away and starting her new job was bothering her.

"I hate it," she said eventually, pausing on the middle of the footbridge, and leaning on the railing. "I feel as if I'm trying to sew a garment but the pattern's torn, and I'm having to make it up as I go. I don't have all the information, and it's freaking me out. I just have to take everyone and everything at face value. It's horrible."

"You can trust me," he said, although as the words left his mouth his stomach roiled uneasily. He hated Noelle at that moment for making him lie to his fiancé.

"Can I?" She turned her large green eyes up to him.

"I'd never knowingly hurt you," he said. "You're the love of my life."

She bit her lip and looked down. Then she turned and carried on walking.

He caught up with her and held out his hand, and she slid hers into it.

"Okay," she said in a jovial tone, obviously deciding to turn the conversation more lighthearted, "so how many girls had you dated before me?"

"Three-hundred-and-twenty-one."

"Christ, Rafe!"

"I'm joking. Jeez."

"I should hope so. So, how many?"

"That's kind of private."

"I thought we didn't have any secrets? You haven't told me before?"

"Might have."

She bumped shoulders with him. "More or less than fifty?"

He gave her an amused look. "I don't know whether to be flattered or insulted by that. A *lot* less than fifty."

"It's a compliment. You're gorgeous." She gave him a curious look. "You must have had tons of girls after you."

"I had a few girlfriends at school. At eighteen I went out with a girl called Nina and we dated about a year. After her, another couple of short-term girlfriends, then there was Tessa. We went out for five years."

Phoebe's eyebrows rose. "That's a long time."

"I guess we both thought we were the one at the time."

"What went wrong?"

"I met you."

"What do you mean?"

"I was living with Tessa when I met you. Not in our house—in a place in Paihia. Looking back, we'd already grown apart. We had our own lives, our own friends. Even if I hadn't met you, I don't think it would have been long before we broke up. You just sped up the process."

"What happened?"

"Elliot introduced us in the bar. He knew I was with Tessa, but he saw the way I looked at you. We sat and talked for an hour. I didn't ask you out right then, because I was with Tessa, but when I went home I couldn't stop thinking about you. For two days, I couldn't sleep. I laid awake those nights on the couch trying to decide what to do. I thought what if I break up with Tessa and ask you out, and you say no? But I knew it wasn't fair on Tessa to do it the other way around. If I was interested in someone else, our relationship was over. So I broke up with her, and, that afternoon, I rang you and asked you out."

"I said yes?"

"You told me you were dating someone else. I said that you weren't, you were dating me." He smirked at the memory.

"You're so arrogant," she said.

"It worked, though. We went to the cinema that night. The rest is history."

She smiled, but her eyes were cautious. "It's a good story. But that's the weird thing—I didn't know it up until now. How do I know you're not hiding anything else from me?"

"I wasn't hiding it, Phoebe. I just hadn't gotten around to telling you."

"Okay, so what else haven't you gotten around to telling me?"

"Probably a billion other things. It's not easy for me either," he said somewhat irritably.

Her expression softened. "I know. I'm sorry."

He pressed the button on his keyring and unlocked the car. "Don't worry about it. Let's go home and I'll make us some dinner. What do you fancy?"

"A curry," she said immediately as she got in. "Something mild but tasty."

"Okay." He got in the driver's side and started the engine.

"With meat," she added, clipping in her belt.

He glanced over at her. "You sure?"

"Definitely."

He didn't say anything, and she frowned at him. "Are you going all judgmental on me?"

"Of course not." He steered the car onto their road. "But I am worried that if and when you get your memory back, you'll blame me for letting you eat meat. Just like you're not sure whether to trust your old self or the new you, I'm not sure either. The old Phoebe would scold me for giving her meat, because I know her feelings on eating it."

"It's my decision," she said. "I'm not going to blame you for anything, Rafe, I swear."

He turned onto their drive and parked the car, deciding it was best not to reply to that. "Come on, then. I'll make a chicken curry."

While he cooked, she sat at her desk and flicked through some of the folders she kept of the dresses that she and Bianca had made, familiarizing herself with their work. Then, after they'd eaten, they watched another movie, sitting side by side on the sofa, holding hands.

By that time, it was nearly eight p.m., and she was looking tired again.

"I think I'm going to have to go to bed," she said.

"That's okay. I'll come with you and have a read. You go ahead—I'll clear up here and join you in a minute."

He finished stacking the dishwasher, closed the windows, and turned off the lights before going into the bedroom. Phoebe was already in bed, and he was conscious of her watching him as he moved around. After visiting the bathroom, he came out in his T-shirt and boxer briefs, put his jeans over the chair, and lowered the spare mattress to the floor.

"Rafe," she said.

He tossed a pillow onto the mattress. "Yeah?"

"It's stupid, you sleeping on the floor. Sleep next to me."

Chapter Twelve

Phoebe watched Rafe put his hands on his hips and purse his lips. "Are you sure?" he asked.

"To sleep," she clarified. "You keep your hands to yourself."

His lips curved up. "While I'm awake. Can't say what I might do when I'm asleep." He pulled the duvet back, slid underneath, and stretched out beside her.

Giving him a wry look, Phoebe rolled onto her side facing him. He rested his head on a hand, and they surveyed each other for a moment.

The duvet lay across his waist, a strip of skin exposed where his T-shirt had ridden up. He smelled heavenly. His eyes held a hint of sultriness, pleasure maybe, that she'd invited him into her bed. Perhaps this hadn't been such a good plan after all.

"Don't get any ideas," she said.

He just smiled.

They were only about a foot apart. If she leaned forward, she would be able to press her lips to his.

She didn't. But she could have.

His tale about the way they'd met had given her a funny feeling inside. He made it sound highly romantic, with their gazes meeting across a crowded room, and him wanting her so much that he'd given up a five-year relationship without a second thought. She was sure it couldn't have been that easy for him. Had Tessa resisted the breakup? Had she cried when he'd said it was over? Surely, she must have been devastated to lose him?

"What?" he asked, amused at her perusal.

"I was wondering whether Tessa cried when you said it was over."

His brow furrowed. "She was upset that it was done. So was I. We'd been together a long time. The end of an era, you know. I don't think she was devastated to lose me, though."

"Why not?"

"I think she'd fallen out of love with me a while before."

"Really?" she said, puzzled.

His expression softened. He reached out a hand and touched the back of his fingers to her cheek. "Not everyone feels about me the way you do."

She swallowed. "How do I feel about you?"

"You love me." He trailed a finger around her ear and down her neck. "You desire me."

"Do I?" Her voice came out as a whisper.

"You do."

"How much?"

His lips curved up, his finger stroking along her collarbone. "We've set this bed alight a few times."

"I wish I could remember," she said wistfully.

His smile faded, and he lowered his hand. "Are you trying to make me cry?"

"I'm sorry."

"It's okay. We'll have to start from the beginning again, that's all. When you're ready."

The breath caught in her throat at the implication. He wanted to make love to her. He was expecting to.

"You might be disappointed," she said.

"Never."

Her face warmed. "I don't remember what to do. I won't know any flash tricks or anything."

"I don't need flash tricks, Phoebe. I only need you."

"But what if you wanted me to do something and I didn't know what it was?"

"Like what?"

"I don't know. A special position or something."

"I'll draw a diagram. Seriously, it's like a riding a bike. It'll come back to you."

She chewed her bottom lip.

"Don't do that," he said.

"Why?"

"Because it turns me on." His voice was low, husky.

She released her lip, her heart thumping on her ribs. "That makes me feel a bit lightheaded," she said, somewhat faintly.

"What does?"

"The thought of turning you on."

"You do it ten times an hour, Phoebe. You'd better get used to it."

She could feel the electricity zinging between them. It almost made her hair rise with static.

"You make me feel funny inside," she said. Her stomach was fluttering, and there was a strange ache between her thighs.

His gaze dropped to her lips. "It's only been a week since we made love, but it feels like a year. I miss you."

"I'm not ready," she said.

"I know. I'm just saying."

"I want to be."

"There's no rush."

She moistened her lips. "I want to kiss you again," she whispered. "But I don't want to be a prick tease."

He laughed at that. "We're getting married," he said with amusement.

"I know. But I don't want to lead you on, it's not fair."

"I'm twenty-nine, not nineteen. I think I can control myself." He tipped his head from side to side and his lips twisted. "Probably." He met her gaze and smiled.

"Will you kiss me?" she asked him.

In answer, he shifted closer to her, so they were only six inches apart.

"I'll do anything you want," he said simply. "I'm yours to command."

"So, if I say go and do the laundry…"

He laughed and lowered his lips to hers.

Phoebe rolled onto her back, lifting her hand to slide into his hair, and felt his hand slip beneath the covers to rest on her ribcage, just beneath her breast. His mouth was warm on hers, his lips firm but gentle, and when she felt the touch of his tongue on her lips, she opened her mouth to give him access.

Ohhh… It was heavenly, lying there in the warm bed, the last rays of the dying sun streaming through the window, being kissed by the most gorgeous guy she was sure she'd ever laid eyes on. She rested her other hand on his back, feeling his muscles through the T-shirt, tempted to slide her fingers beneath the cotton and touch his warm skin, but she resisted.

He took his time kissing her, his hand stroking over her hip and down her thigh, pulling her close to him, almost subconsciously, she thought, as if his body hungered for hers. Making love with him would be amazing, she knew it instinctively. She burned inside at the thought of his lips on her skin, his fingers teasing her toward the height of pleasure. She wished she could remember having sex with him. How would it feel to have a man inside her, to have his eyes on her when she came? To watch him come inside her?

She ached for it, but her head hurt, and she was tired, and she still wasn't ready to give herself to an almost stranger, not yet. As if sensing her thoughts, Rafe lifted his head, and he gave her a small smile.

"Sorry," she whispered.

He kissed her forehead and slid down a little, gathering her into his arms. "Come here."

She rolled onto her side, cuddling up to him, and he wrapped his arms around her.

"You make me feel safe," she said. "Is it weird that I trust you, even though I feel I hardly know you?"

He didn't say anything, and she lifted her head to look at him. He was frowning, but as he felt her gaze on him, he looked at her and smiled. "I don't think so. I think some part of you remembers."

She shifted, still feeling an unsatisfied ache between her thighs. "Which part is that?"

He laughed. "Go to sleep."

Resting her hand on his ribs, she felt the rise and fall of his chest, the deep thud of his heart, and closed her eyes.

In seconds, she was asleep.

*

When she awoke the next day, the bed was empty. For a moment, she wondered if she'd imagined Rafe sleeping beside her. But he'd been there in the night when she'd roused, sprawled on his back, snoring very slightly, taking up too much of the bed, tangled in the covers. She'd lain there for a while watching him. While he was asleep, some of his radiance dimmed, and she didn't feel as blinded by him as when he was awake. He was like the sun, full of so much energy, and with such a big personality that she felt as if she stood in the gigantic shadow he cast. Had she always felt that way?

Wondering where he was now, she rose from the bed, stood, and stretched in front of the window. She felt better today. At that moment, her head wasn't hurting, and the bumps and bruises on her body weren't as sore. She fancied a hot bath and some breakfast, then she thought she might feel almost normal.

Leaving the room, she wandered through the kitchen and poured herself a glass of water. Hearing noises in the spare room, she walked through and paused in the doorway.

He was working out again. This time, he was lying on his back on a bench, lifting weights. Phoebe leaned on the doorjamb, sipping her water, and watched him. His biceps bunched and flexed as he lowered the metal bar with the huge weights on either end, then pushed it slowly up until his arms were straight. She wouldn't be able to lift even one of those weights. Sweat dampened his tee and his hair, and he gave a sexy grunt each time he pushed up. Jeez. What was wrong with her? All she could think about was getting her hands on this guy and touching him up.

Muttering to herself, she backed away silently and went back to the bedroom. She was recovering from a brain injury. The last thing she should be thinking about was getting down and dirty with a sexy firefighter.

She bathed and dressed, and, by the time she came out, he was in the kitchen, making coffee. He pushed a cup over to her, and she took it, trying not to eye his damp torso.

"I know, I know," he said. "I'm sweaty and disgusting."

"Totally," she said. She met his eye, and they both started laughing.

"I'll shower in a minute," he said. Leaning a hip against the counter, he took a mouthful of coffee. "How did you sleep?"

"Very well." *Thanks to you.* She was sure that having him by her side had played a big part in that. He'd held her for a long time, and once or twice she'd roused to feel him stroking her back. How had that felt as intimate as when he'd kissed her?

"Good," he said. "You look better this morning."

"I feel better. A bit less achy and tired."

"What would you like to do today?"

"I don't mind. I thought maybe you could suggest somewhere nice we'd been, you know, for memory triggers."

His gaze moved over her shoulder, and she knew he was flicking back through his memories like swiping through a camera roll on his phone. He would be remembering places they'd been, things they'd done together. When had he first told her he loved her? Where had they first had sex? It must be hard for him that she couldn't remember.

It might have made other men angry or resentful, but he'd only been patient with her, and understanding.

Yet another reason he made her melt.

His gaze came back to her, and he smiled. "We had a lovely day at Waitangi once. It's supposed to be nice weather today, so it'll be lovely up there. Fancy going?"

"That sounds great."

"Okay." He finished off his coffee. "I'll hop in the shower." He slid the mug toward the sink and his eyes gleamed. "Want to scrub my back?"

"Pass," she said, although she was severely tempted.

He just grinned and walked off. She watched him go, her gaze lingering on his tight butt. It would be so easy to give in to his subtle persuasion and sleep with him. She had no doubt he'd be gentle, and that it would be wonderful. But she mustn't do that until she was sure she was going to stay with him. It was still far too early to make any decisions. She couldn't marry him just because he was gorgeous and she wanted to get into his boxers. The Phoebe she'd become after her father had died might have been the perfect fit for this guy, but what about the Phoebe she was now? How could she be sure they were compatible?

Resolving to think about it later, she rang her mother, who reminded her that she had a doctor's appointment that afternoon, and chatted to her until Rafe came out, and then she gathered her purse, slipped her feet into her sandals, and followed him out to the car.

It took them about twenty minutes to get to Waitangi, and Rafe played some music as he drove, saying these were some of their favorite songs. He sang along, and Phoebe listened, loving his voice, but she didn't remember any of the tunes. How odd that everything had been erased from her brain, as if all her memories were folders in a filing cabinet that had been torched, leaving nothing but a heap of twisted metal and ash.

Did it mean that all the feelings she'd had for Rafe were nothing but groups of neurons that had been dislodged with a simple bump? Was the way he made her feel now an echo of how she'd felt, or was she just being fanciful and pretending the connection between them was deep and meaningful when in fact it was nothing more than an animal sexual attraction?

"Stop worrying," he said.

"I'm not."

"Yes, you are. I know you well enough."

"You knew old Phoebe."

"She's not that different to new Phoebe."

"Isn't she?" she pressed. "Am I exactly the same?"

He signaled as he slowed at the roundabout, but Phoebe was too agitated to appreciate the beauty of the Pacific Ocean ahead of her, sparkling in the sun.

"No," he said eventually as he pulled away.

"I know I'm not. I can't be without all the experiences I've had over the last eight years. I'm not the person you fell in love with, Rafe. How can you be sure we're still compatible?"

He drove over the bridge toward the Waitangi Treaty House, into the car park, and slid the car into a space. He put the handbrake on and switched off the engine. Then he unclipped his seatbelt and turned in the seat to face her.

"Stop stressing," he said.

"I can't help it."

"I know, and I understand, but you're going to drive yourself crazy trying to second guess yourself all the time."

"I hate it," she said, her heart racing. "I hate that I don't remember you, or what we did, or what kind of person I've become. I don't understand that woman at all. How can I not eat meat? I love a good steak! And bacon! How can I not eat bacon anymore?"

"It's not set in stone, Phoebe. If you want to start eating bacon, you can."

"The bacon's not the issue," she said, somewhat hysterically. "I can't even comprehend how I couldn't like bacon. It makes no sense to me at all."

"Look," Rafe said gently. "If you were to draw a diagram of our lives, it would be full of choices and decisions. That's what the alternate universe theory is all about—that there are an infinite number of universes where every choice we've ever made is played out. Some of the choices are tiny—which car you bought, whether you decided to go out or stay in on a particular day. And some are big. Your father dying was one of the bigger crossroads. You could have reacted to that in a variety of ways. You went down one particular road, and branched off. Now, it's just as if you're back at that crossroads. You're still the same person, the girl I fell in love with."

She looked into his eyes, trying to quell the panic that was threatening to engulf her. "I know you're right," she whispered. "It's nothing to worry about. But it's as if I'm looking down into a deep well, and I can see something glittering on the bottom like a coin, but I can't quite make it out. There's something just out of my reach… Something I feel I need to remember, and I can't get to it. I don't know what to do, Rafe. I feel like I'm going mad."

Chapter Thirteen

Rafe's stomach knotted, and for a moment the truth hovered on his lips, ready to spill like frozen peas from a bag. But Noelle's firm words echoed in his head, *just let her heal*, as well as the look in her eyes, almost of panic. She was really afraid that the truth would set her daughter back, and he could understand that. But it was so hard keeping it from her.

Just a few more days, he promised himself. Phoebe was already looking better. Even forty-eight hours would help. He had to keep her as calm as he could until then, and support her through this difficult time.

"Your brain is trying to mend the lost connections," he told her. "I know it's hard, and you want all the answers now, but you just need to give yourself time."

Her green eyes met his, her chest rising and falling quickly with her rapid breaths. "I'm sorry. I'm full of such conflicting emotions. Like with you. I feel such a strong attraction to you, and it's difficult to fight it, but I know I have to, because I can't remember our relationship, or how I felt about you, I mean it would be so easy to give in to it, but maybe I'll get my memory back and I'll be angry with myself for saying or doing something, and then I'll—"

Sliding a hand to the side of her head without the wound, he leaned forward and captured her lips with his.

Phoebe gave a brief, muffled protest, but Rafe didn't release her. Instead, he tipped his head to the side, slanting his lips across hers, and brushed her bottom lip with his tongue. A small moan sounded deep in her throat, and then she opened her mouth and returned the kiss, leaning into him.

Rafe didn't hold back this time, pouring out his passion, his heartache, and his fear that he was going to lose her, pulling her tightly against him. Leaving her lips briefly, he kissed up her cheekbone to her ear, sliding his hand to her breast and cupping it, brushing his thumb over her nipple. She gasped, and he moved his hand beneath her breast and pressed it over her ribs.

"I can feel your heart racing," he said fiercely. "You can't fake that, Phoebe. It doesn't matter what memories you have or whether you think you've changed—you want me, and I want you, and that's all that matters."

"You make me ache," she whispered.

He kissed back to her mouth and brushed his lips against hers. "I know a great remedy for that."

She closed her eyes. "Oh God, don't…"

"I'll show you tonight," he said, running the tip of his tongue along her bottom lip.

"It must mean something, the way I feel about you." She slid a hand into his hair, her nails scraping his scalp.

"Your soul remembers me. It's like memory foam. It's shaped itself to me, and now we fit together perfectly."

"I almost believe that," she whispered.

He touched his nose to hers. "It's the truth. I've won you once already, and I'm not going to let you go without a fight, Phoebe Goldsmith. If you think I'm going to take a back seat and be passive in this relationship, you've got another think coming."

"I don't think you know the meaning of the word passive."

His lips curved up. "I don't know—you've tied me to the bed before."

Her eyes widened, and she moved back a little. "Seriously?"

"Hell, yeah."

"Oh my God. Have you… um… tied me down?"

"Many, many times."

Her lips parted, and a flush appeared in her cheeks.

"That surprises you?" he said, amused.

"I… hadn't thought about it before. So, we're not… lights out, missionary position kind of people?"

He laughed softly and twirled a strand of her hair around his finger. "Not in the slightest." He kissed the piece of hair. "You're very adventurous in the bedroom."

He could see the curiosity and excitement in her eyes. "In what way?" she asked.

"You love trying new positions. Roleplay. Toys."

"Like Lego?" she joked weakly.

"No, Phoebe, like things that buzz in your private places. I know every inch of your body," he murmured, winding the strand of hair tighter around his finger, so she had to move closer to him. "I know how to tease you right to the edge of passion and keep you there for hours. You like me doing that." Jesus, he should stop now, he was turning himself on and he had a hard-on he was going to have trouble getting rid of, but her eyes were wide and excited, her beautiful lips soft and parted, and he couldn't stop himself. "You want me to tell you what part of your body you like me to tease with my finger while you come?"

She was barely breathing. "You mean…"

"I do, Phoebe, my beautiful sex goddess."

Her cheeks flushed scarlet. "Oh God. You're so wicked."

"It's your fault. I was Mr. Nice Guy before I met you." There was some truth in the words. His early sexual experiences had been unremarkable, and Tessa hadn't been keen on experimenting too much in the bedroom. Phoebe had been open to exploration, though, and together they'd done practically everything a couple could do together.

"You're teasing me," she whispered.

"No. You've corrupted me, sweetheart. I go only where you lead me."

"I'm not like that."

"You are. You're the most passionate woman I've ever met."

"Stop it," she said, pink and agitated. "I don't believe you. You're making it sound as if I tell you what to do all the time. There's no way you're that docile. You're more like a feral tomcat."

"I'm really not."

"You expect me to believe you're submissive in bed?"

"I'm stronger than you. That's led to some fun moments."

"Rafe!"

"What?"

"Stop telling me about rude things we've done. You're making me all flustered."

"Aw," he said, kissing the corner of her mouth, "you love it."

"I don't."

"Push me away, then."

"I'm trying. You're like a brick wall."

He chuckled. "Look at you, blushing like a girl on her first date."

"It feels like my first date, Rafe! I don't remember going to bed with you, let alone getting up to… whatever we get up to!" Turning, she opened the car door and got out.

Sighing, he got out quickly, locked the car, and ran after her. Catching up to her, he took her hand and tugged her to a stop.

"Come here." He pulled her into his arms. She went stiff for a moment, then buried her face in his T-shirt. "I'm sorry." He kissed the top of her head. "I didn't mean to embarrass you."

"It's just so weird, and so unfair." Her voice came out muffled against his shirt. "It's like something out of a science fiction movie. I feel as if I've been abducted by aliens or something."

"I am sorry, sweetheart."

"No, it's not your fault. I feel sorry for you." She turned her face to rest her cheek on his chest. "Relationships take time to build and develop, and now you have to go back to square one. You were marrying this girl who knew you intimately, and she just vanished overnight." She swallowed hard and moved back to look up at him. "I… I wouldn't blame you if you wanted to call it off. The wedding, I mean. It's not all about whether I want it to happen. If you've changed your mind, I'll understand."

He cupped her face. "I haven't changed my mind. You might not remember what we had, but it is worth fighting for. We weren't just in love, Phoebe. We were wildly, madly, passionately in love. I still am. I'm obsessed by you. You mean everything to me. Do you really think I'd just walk away from that?"

"You did before," she said. "With Tessa."

That stung. "I didn't feel a tenth—a hundredth—for Tessa what I feel about you," he said sharply. "I drifted into that relationship; we both did. She would say the same if you asked her. We were like… I don't know… A log fire on a cool evening. When you look at me across a room, fireworks go off in my head. When I kiss you, the blood in my veins turns to lava. You heat me up from the inside out, and I think I made you feel the same way. I'm not giving up on that."

Her green eyes glistened. "What if I never feel about you the same way I once did?"

His stomach clenched in fear, but he kept his gaze fixed on hers. "I don't believe that's going to happen."

"You're mighty sure of yourself." A touch of the old Phoebe flashed in her eyes—she was taunting him, flirting with him without realizing it.

"I'm sure of us." He moved a little closer to her, ignoring the tourists around them walking to the treaty house. He ached to hold her, to have her look at him the way she used to. "Tell me you don't feel anything for me at all. Tell me that when I look at you, when I tell you how I want to strip off your dress and kiss down your body and pleasure you with my tongue, that you don't feel a thing."

Her lips parted, her eyes taking on a look of helplessness that filled him with joy. "I can't," she whispered.

"Then I'll wait," he said. "I don't care how long it takes, until you're ready." He kissed her.

When he eventually lifted his head, her eyes were closed, and she gave a dreamy sigh. "I think you've slipped something in my drink," she whispered.

He smiled. "Not quite. Now come on, before I take you back to the car and do unmentionable things to you."

He led her into the building, and they spent half an hour wandering around the museum because she didn't remember it being built. They studied the displays that told the story of the Europeans' arrival in New Zealand, and the creation of the Treaty between them and Maori, along with the issues surrounding some of its wording that continued to cause problems.

After that, they took the wooden walkway through the bush, listening to the tuis and kererus calling in the ferns that arched above their heads, and then went up to the large lawn where the flagstaff marked the place where the Treaty was signed. There was a beautiful view right across the Bay of Islands, and Rafe took her to the far side. They could see an ocean liner visiting the bay, and a hundred fishing boats making their way to and from Paihia and Russell.

He stopped her there and turned to face her. "This is where I first said I love you."

Her eyebrows rose. "Really?"

"Right here. I'll say it again now. I love you, Phoebe Goldsmith. Whatever happens over the next week or two, remember that. I want to stand in front of our family and friends and promise to love you for the rest of my life."

She blinked a few times, then opened her mouth and said "I—"

He put a finger to her lips. "Don't say it because you feel sorry for me."

Her expression softened. "I don't deserve you."

"You don't know how many times I've said that to you. I'm nothing special, sweetheart." He took her hand. "Come on. It's a beautiful day. Let's have a walk around and then we'll go back to the car. I don't want you to get too tired."

Chapter Fourteen

They spent the rest of the morning exploring Waitangi, had some lunch in the cafe, and then called in at the doctor's surgery on the way home for her appointment.

"Hello, Phoebe." Dr. Angus McGregor smiled at her as she came into the room. He was a tall, slender guy with short brown hair and a kind face. He was probably only early thirties, she thought, but he had a very young face. He also had a mild Scottish accent that had presumably mellowed after years spent in New Zealand. "It's good to see you. I've been so worried."

She took the seat next to his desk. Rafe had told her that Angus was not only her doctor but a close friend with whom they sometimes went out socially. Yet another person who knew intimate details about her, but whom she didn't remember.

"Um… thank you." She cleared her throat. "I should point out that I'm very sorry, but I don't remember you." It was becoming a common phrase.

His expression softened. "That's okay. I was so sorry to hear about your accident. How are you feeling?"

"I'm okay, physically anyway. As well as can be expected."

"Let's check you over, shall we?"

He took her blood pressure and temperature, then spent some time looking at her bumps and grazes. Finally, he said, "Let's have a look at the wound."

She turned in the seat, drew her hair aside, and let him peel away the dressing. She felt his fingers prodding gently.

"It looks very good." He went over to a drawer and retrieved a clean dressing. "Considering the accident was only five days ago, it's healing well." He wiped around the wound, peeled the backing off the dressing, and placed it carefully. "Your hair is already growing back. I think after this dressing comes off, you'll probably be all right leaving it open as it's not weeping. How are the headaches?"

She lowered her hair over it, and watched him sit back down. "Manageable, with the pills they gave me. A lot better than they were the first day."

"Good. Now, you said 'physically anyway'," he commented. "How are you doing otherwise? How are you sleeping?"

"The first couple of nights were very restless, but I've been better since…"

He raised an eyebrow.

"Since I shared a bed with Rafe," she admitted, her face warming.

Angus just nodded. "And mentally? Emotionally?"

"I don't know. I feel… confused a lot of the time. It takes me ages to process my thoughts."

"That's perfectly understandable, and nothing to be worried about." She hesitated, and he leaned forward, his elbows on his knees. "What is it, Phoebe?"

"Rafe said you're a good friend."

"That's true. I'm giving you away at your wedding." He smiled.

She stared at him. "Oh! I didn't realize that!"

"Well, what with your father having passed away last year… I spent a lot of time with you and your family. I know I'm not exactly your father's age," and his lips twisted, "but you asked me because Elliot is Rafe's best man, and Dominic is performing the ceremony."

She shifted on the chair. "It feels a bit odd. I'm not sure I feel comfortable, you know, talking about… stuff."

His smile faded. "If you'd rather see someone else, I understand. It must be very difficult for you at the moment, not knowing who to trust."

"That's exactly it."

"I can only imagine. All I can say is that I've been your doctor since I started practicing here. I'm your doctor first and foremost, and anything you say in here is strictly confidential." He tipped his head to the side. "Is this about Rafe?"

"Yes. No. Sort of."

"Well, that clears that up." He smiled.

She looked at her hands. "We're supposed to be getting married in a week."

"Are you having second thoughts?"

"I don't know what to think. I wish it was more than seven days away, so I had more time. But everything's booked, and Rafe would be so disappointed if I postponed it."

"You have to think about what's best for you," Angus said gently. "But I know that doesn't come naturally to you."

She surveyed him, feeling for a moment as if she was lost in a maze in the mist, with no hope of seeing the way out. "How would you describe me? As a person?"

"Smart. Driven. Confident. Funny."

"You've seen us together. Me and Rafe?"

"Of course."

"I know this is a strange question, but what's our relationship like?"

It wasn't really the sort of question she should be asking her doctor, but she wanted an honest answer, not what her family thought she wanted to hear.

"When you're in the room, Rafe can't take his eyes off you," Angus said. "When you're apart, you're all he talks about. I've known him for a long time, and I've never seen him like this with anyone else."

Warmth spread through her. It was one thing for Rafe to tell her this, but another for someone else to confirm it. "And what am I like with him?"

"You love to tease him. You flirt with him all the time, pushing his buttons. There's a lot of electricity between the two of you."

"Did I change much after my father died?"

He tipped his head from side to side. "You became more serious. Quieter. Your fitness levels increased by about eighty percent."

"What was Rafe's reaction to that?"

"He supported you all the way, from what I could see. I really don't think you have any worries there. But I can see that something's bothering you."

She sucked her bottom lip. "It's just a gut feeling, but I have nothing to base it on. I do trust him. I suppose the question is do I trust myself? Do I carry on with my life believing that the decisions I've made are the right ones? At the moment, I have no desire to continue training. And the thought of committing myself to a man I've only just met seems crazy. But I find myself drawn to him in spite of that. When he's in the room, it's as if he shines so brightly I can't see anything else. I know that sounds overly romantic, but it's true. And I don't know if that's because of what we had, or just because he's such a strong character."

"Well, I don't feel like that when he's in the room," Angus said, and smiled. "We know so little about memory. It's possible that those connections with the past are still stored somewhere in your brain. Who knows if you remember Rafe in other ways?"

She rubbed her nose. "He said I've had an IUD fitted."

Angus checked the screen. "Yes. About a year ago. A hormonal one. You told me you like it because your periods are light-to-nonexistent, which is useful when you're running a lot."

"How is my health in general?"

"Excellent. I've only seen you here a couple of times. Once for a chest infection after a cold. Once to check on a mole, which was fine."

"So… with this in mind…" She touched the back of her head. "Is there any reason I shouldn't… you know… with Rafe…" Her face burned.

Angus gave a small smile. "Of course not. The most important thing at the moment is for you to relax. I'm sure lovemaking would help with that."

She examined her hands, embarrassed.

"Just remember that anything you feel is normal," he said. "It's common to have a decreased sex drive after a brain injury, and some people have trouble becoming aroused, and may be unable to reach a climax. Sex engages all of our senses, and it's not unusual for your feelings to change."

She swallowed hard, not sure if she wanted to know that.

"Nothing's set in stone," he said hurriedly. "My best advice would be to do what feels right. Don't let Rafe or anyone else push you into anything you're not ready for. You have all the time in the world to get better. You could have been killed, Phoebe. But you weren't, you're here and you're alive, and that's wonderful. It doesn't matter if it takes six months or a year for you to return to your old life, and it doesn't matter if you never do. You can't live old Phoebe's life for her. Today is all that matters. Follow your heart, and you won't go far wrong."

*

"What did Angus say?" Rafe asked when they were back in the car, and he was driving her home.

"I'm doing as well as can be expected. He told me I mustn't have sex for at least six months." She looked at him, and burst out laughing at the look on his face.

He gave her a wry look and returned his gaze to the road. "You're such a tease."

"He did tell me to take my time, and only do what I'm ready for."

"That sounds like good advice."

She looked out of the window. *You can't live old Phoebe's life for her.* It *was* good advice. No second guessing, or worrying about what she would or wouldn't have done before. *Today is all that matters. Follow your heart, and you won't go far wrong.* Angus was right. All she had was her gut feeling, and she was going to trust that and do what felt right.

When they got in, Rafe directed her to the bedroom, saying she looked tired, and she didn't argue. She fell asleep quickly, and to her relief, she didn't dream, and awoke refreshed and feeling brighter.

Dominic rang, and she chatted to him for a while, and then not long after, Roberta called to see how she was getting on. Phoebe kept the conversation light, pleased to hear from her, but she was conscious that her twin hadn't yet rung her. She found it unsettling, because in the past when they weren't together they were contacting each other constantly. Bianca must really resent her leaving to get another job, she thought sadly. She was going to have to talk to her about it at some point. Maybe in a couple of days, when Rafe went back on day shift. She'd have more time to herself then to see her friends and family, and make her final decision for the wedding the following week.

That evening, she and Rafe cooked dinner together, which was fun, and after they'd eaten, they cuddled up on the sofa to watch another movie.

"I don't mind if you want to go out with your mates or something," she said as he scrolled through to find something they would both enjoy.

"I'm happy here, with you," he said. "And don't think I've forgotten our conversation earlier today. I still intend to show you my stress remedy." He gave her an amused glance.

She inhaled as her heart skipped a beat. "I told you, Angus said no sex for six months."

"Well, a) I don't believe you, b) I don't even think he's a real doctor, and c) I know you better than he does. You have a high sex drive and you need to let off steam. It's purely medicinal."

"Jesus."

"One orgasm, twice a day. He would've written you a prescription for it if he could."

She pushed him. "Stop talking about sex and choose a movie."

He chuckled and picked one. "Okay. But come here. I want a cuddle."

Unable to resist him, she let him pull her to his side, and rested her head on his shoulder. It was as if he were a magnet and she were made of iron, drawn to him by forces beyond her control. Was she stupid to fight them? He was so gorgeous, and he smelled so good…

You have a high sex drive and you need to let off steam. It was true that she felt on edge, and she couldn't deny that the thought of getting intimate with him excited her. But it worried her a little that Angus had also said her injury might affect her ability to get aroused or have a climax. Maybe the tension that an orgasm brought with it would increase her headache. She didn't know what was normal, or what she was expected to feel. How was she supposed to negotiate this tricky maze of feelings?

They watched the movie, and she felt him glance at her from time to time, and knew she was being quiet. When he turned off the TV, she half expected him to query her about it, but he didn't. He told her to get ready for bed while he turned out the lights and locked the doors, and so she went to the bathroom, put on the T-shirt of his she'd been wearing to bed, and slid under the covers, her heart racing when he came into the bedroom.

He went to the bathroom, and she heard him cleaning his teeth. Then he came out and dropped his jeans over the chair in the corner. She watched him walk toward the bed, admiring his butt and thighs in his boxer briefs, and the way the sleeves of his T-shirt clung to his powerful biceps. He slipped beneath the duvet, and, just like the night before, he stretched out beside her and propped his head on a hand.

"Okay," he said. "What's bothering you?"

Chapter Fifteen

Phoebe's eyes glistened, and Rafe saw her bite her bottom lip hard, trying not to let them fall.

"Hey." He frowned and reached out a hand to cup her face. "Why are you upset? Is it because I teased you? I thought you realized I was joking. You've had a brain injury, for Christ's sake—I'm not going to try anything on. Don't be scared."

"I'm sorry if I've been quiet this evening, but it's not because I'm scared. Quite the opposite. I think about you all the time, Rafe. I can't stop thinking about you. About going to bed with you. I know I shouldn't; I should wait until I'm better, and until my memory comes back, but every time you look at me, my body heats up, and there's nothing I can do about it."

He kissed her nose, his heart picking up speed. "That's sweet, but it's out of the question."

"It's not. I talked to Angus about it."

He raised an eyebrow. "Seriously?"

"He said there's no problem with having sex as long as I'm ready. But the thing is, he said that with a brain injury sometimes things change. It can affect… you know… the libido, and whether you can get aroused, and I'm worried about what will happen, because I don't know what to expect and I don't want to disappoint you, and—"

Rafe stopped her with a kiss. Phoebe mumbled something and put a hand on his chest to push him away, but he took it, linked their fingers, and held it tightly. In the end, she went limp and let him kiss her. He did so slowly, dipping his tongue into her mouth, and she sighed and squirmed beneath him, pressing her thighs together in a way that told him how aroused she was. She'd been thinking about sex all evening. That was why she'd been quiet.

He lifted his head. "We're not having sex, Phoebe, I don't care what Angus said."

The disappointment on her face almost made him cave, but even if she was ready for it, he wasn't. He wanted her, but not like this, with so many secrets between them.

But that didn't mean he couldn't give her pleasure. He could see she was worried that the injury had affected her. Well, he'd soon put her mind at rest.

"Roll onto your side," he said.

She pursed her lips, not moving. In reply, he pushed her away from him, moving up close behind her so she couldn't roll back.

"You haven't changed," he murmured in her ear. "I know you, Phoebe Goldsmith. I can see right into your heart. You're still the same woman I fell in love with. Your body remembers me, even if your mind doesn't."

"But we're not having sex?"

"No."

Her face had flushed pink. "You're turning me down?"

"I'm going to give you an orgasm. We're going to take our time, so you can see that everything is normal, and that you feel okay afterward, and there's nothing to worry about."

"What if I say no to that?"

"You won't, because you like orgasms, and you're all tense and need to relax."

"I don't know why you think you have the last word in the bedroom. You're not the boss of me, Rafe Masters."

"Absolutely I am. Always have been, always will be, and you like it that way."

"I don't."

"Yes, you do." He put an arm over her and held her tightly as she tried to push him away. "Stop fidgeting."

She wriggled. "Stop bossing me about."

"I'll tie you down if I have to."

She gasped. "You wouldn't!"

"I would. You forget that we've done this a thousand times, and I know you inside out. You like to fight me. But you want me to take charge."

"Maybe I've changed. Maybe I don't like that anymore."

"Our safe word is heartbeat," he murmured, kissing her neck. "Say heartbeat and I'll stop. Otherwise… I'm in charge, and you'll do as I say." His lifted his head and waited.

She looked over her shoulder and met his gaze. "Have I ever said it?"

His lips curved up. "No."

She shivered. "I'm not taking off the T-shirt."

He chuckled. "Like that's going to stop me." Placing a finger at the nape of her neck, he trailed it down her back over the cotton. She closed her eyes and sighed, going limp again in his arms.

He kissed her head, above the hair covering the dressing. "How is your head feeling?"

"It's okay. I feel… fuzzy. I'm tired of thinking. It makes it hurt."

"Then don't. Just feel." He placed kisses slowly down her neck and over her shoulder. "Imagine we're on a desert island somewhere, under the shade of a palm tree, and it's hot, and there's nobody else around." He brushed his lips along her arm, touching his tongue occasionally to her skin. "There's just me and you and the seagulls in the sky, and the waves in the distance. We can do anything here, and there's nobody to see, and nobody to judge. Just me and you. We have all the time in the world to love each other."

"Oh God…" She shuddered as he continued drawing patterns on her back. "I wish I was stronger, but I can't resist you…"

"We're getting married. You don't have to resist me." He rested his fingers under her arm and drew them down her ribs, over her hips and along the outside of her thigh. "Imagine lying naked on the beach, feeling the sun on your skin." He brought his fingers back up, sliding them under the T-shirt. Beneath the cotton, she was wearing a pair of panties, but he could feel that she didn't have a bra on. He brushed his fingers over her tummy, and she moaned in response.

"You've always been so easy to arouse," he said, drawing circles up her ribs to beneath her breasts. "Sex with you is always amazing."

"I wish I could remember," she whispered.

"You'll have new memories to replace the old soon enough." He shifted behind her, sliding his left arm beneath her shoulders, and moved her so she was half lying on him, her back to his chest. "Look at me."

She turned her head, her sultry eyes half lidded, her lips parted, and he kissed her, moving his left hand beneath the T-shirt to cup her breast.

"How does this feel?" he murmured, brushing his thumb over her nipple.

"Mmm... nice..."

He touched his tongue to her bottom lip, and she arched her back to kiss him, unwittingly pushing her breast into his hand. He tried not to groan out loud, turned on himself, his erection pressing in the small of her back, eager for action. She was hot for him, and she'd never needed hours of foreplay. Normally, she'd be begging him to slide inside her by now, maybe even pushing him onto his back so she could sit astride him, and he'd let her have her own way for a while before rolling her onto her back so he could thrust home. Their lovemaking was sometimes slow and sensual, sometimes fast and furious, and he loved the way she challenged him, wanting him to fight back and take charge. They were perfectly matched, and he couldn't believe the accident had changed the way she was deep down.

But that was for him to explore another night. For now, he just wanted to give her pleasure and put her mind at ease. Her nipple was like soft velvet, but he could feel it hardening, turning to a tight bud, and she moaned as he tugged it, making it lengthen in his fingers.

"Just relax," he murmured, hoping Angus was right and any tensing of her muscles wouldn't affect her head. "Let it happen. Don't reach for it."

She kissed him again, and he felt her gasp against his lips as he traced the fingers of his right hand down her thigh, then up over her panties.

"Do you want me to touch you here?" he whispered, brushing very lightly between her legs.

"Mmm." She groaned as he tugged her nipple again. "Yes..."

He moved his hand down to her knee and lifted it, pulling her leg across him, and leaving her exposed to his touch. Then he slid his fingers down, over the top of the cotton panties, touching ever so lightly between her legs. She shuddered.

"Steady." He stroked the inside of her thighs, then back up between her legs. "Does that feel nice?"

"Oh... yes..."

"Do you think you've changed, Phoebe? Do you think I'm going to have trouble bringing you to orgasm?"

She groaned. "You're so fucking arrogant."

"I should make you wait for swearing at me."

"I would've thought you'd like that." Her green eyes flashed at him briefly.

"I do. Swear all you like." He ran his finger underneath the elastic of her panties, making her stomach ripple. "We both like talking dirty."

"I don't."

"Yes, you do." He kissed her jaw and the corner of her mouth as he brushed his finger over her mound. "You love it when I tell you how I'm going to fuck you."

"Rafe!"

He slid his finger down into the heart of her, and she moaned.

"My Phoebe," he said fiercely as he found her swollen and wet, more than ready for him. It was only then that he realized how worried he'd been that the accident had changed her. But it hadn't. She was still his fiancée, the one who made his heart soar. "Jesus, I love you so much." He slipped his finger down into her, gathering her moisture, then brought it up to start caressing her clit. "I'm going to make you come now."

"Oh God…" She rocked her hips a little against his hand.

"Take it easy," he scolded. "Just let it happen. Don't rush to get there. I'll take you. Let me guide you."

She lifted a hand to slide into his hair, bringing his mouth down to hers as his fingers slipped through her folds, teasing her closer to the edge with every stroke.

"You know…" she whispered, "exactly where to touch me…"

"Of course I do. You're my girl. And I'm never letting you go." His heart was racing, and he plunged his tongue into her mouth, swirling his finger over her clit.

Her fingers tightened in his hair, her hips tilting up. He lifted his head, seeing her cheeks flush, her breathing turn irregular. "Careful," he murmured, slowing his finger, giving her long, even strokes as her climax crept up on her. "That's it. Come for me, sweetheart. Nice and slow."

Her teeth tugged on her bottom lip as her hips stilled. "*Ohhh…*"

He saw it sweep over her, heard her gasps, watched her body tense with pleasure as she clenched deep inside. He'd kept it as slow and gentle as possible, and when her eyes finally fluttered open, he was relieved to see her lips curve up.

"Mmm," she murmured, relaxing in his arms.

He kissed her, taking his time, letting her drift back to earth. When he finally lifted his head, he could see she was almost asleep.

"No pain?" he whispered, touching her head.

"No pain." She blinked slowly, looking into his eyes. "Thank you."

"You're very welcome. I told you we wouldn't have a problem."

She moistened her lips. "Are you sure you don't want to just… climb on board?"

He chuckled and kissed her forehead, removing his arm from beneath her so she could lie properly on her side. "Not tonight. You need sleep."

"What about you?"

"I'm a big boy. I'll manage."

Her eyelids fluttered shut. "I owe you one."

"Don't worry, I'll keep a tally."

Her lips curved up.

Within two minutes, her breathing had turned even.

Rafe waited a bit longer, not wanting to wake her, then rose quietly from the bed and went into the bathroom.

He was still hard as a rock, and there was no way he was going to sleep with an erection like that. Pushing the door to, he slid his hand into his boxers and took himself in hand. He was so keyed up, it took him less than a minute of replaying Phoebe's orgasm in his head before everything tightened and he came with hot, hard pulses that made him grit his teeth so he didn't cry out.

*

In the bed, Phoebe heard his muffled groan. He hadn't been able to resist. Smiling, she snuggled down into the pillows and drifted off to sleep.

Chapter Sixteen

"So, my last day off," Rafe said. "What would you like to do today?"

Phoebe crunched her toast, trying to avert her mind from the thought of staying in bed with him the whole day. He sipped his coffee, his bright blue eyes holding a touch of amusement that told her he knew perfectly well what she was thinking.

It was difficult to turn her mind to anything else. She was sure that last night had been something they'd probably done a hundred times before, and was nothing special in the big scheme of things, but for her, it was the first time she could remember a man touching her that way, and it had blown her mind.

He'd known exactly what to do, what speed and pressure to give her the ultimate pleasure, and all her remaining doubts had fled. This man knew her intimately, maybe even knew her body better than she did. She couldn't deny it any longer. What was the point in turning her back on this relationship? She'd loved him enough to want to marry him. He was an easy man to love—it wouldn't be long, she was sure, before they were back to where they'd left off. She was halfway there already, captivated by his easy charm, his confidence, his assurance of how he felt about her.

"Stop it," he scolded. "Don't look at me like that."

"After last night? I can't help it."

He blew out a breath. "You sure don't make it easy on a guy."

"Aw. Poor Rafe. Getting married to a girl who has the hots for him. What a terrible life you must lead."

He leaned back and pushed away his coffee cup, giving her an exasperated look. "So, getting back to the original question, what would you like to do today?"

Her smile faded a little. She picked up her toast and examined it, then put it down again. "I don't know. I'm disappointed that nowhere I've been has jogged my memory at all. Every now and then I think I can see a shape through the fog, but it goes so quickly. Is there anywhere else you could take me that might help?"

"There are lots of places. I don't want to tire you out, though."

"I don't care. It's more important to me that I remember."

He nodded. "One thing I did wonder was whether you wanted to come to Marlin's tonight. The bar in town. We often meet up there with our friends, and they're all going down there this evening. I originally said we'd pass as I didn't think you'd want to answer a hundred questions, but after what you said, maybe it wouldn't be the worst thing in the world to see everyone."

The thought terrified her, but she could see his point. "What time?"

"Seven-ish."

"Okay. Let's do that. So, what shall we do for the rest of the day?"

"We'll go out," he said. "I'll take you to some of the lovely places we've been, and you can see if it helps the fog to clear."

They got ready and headed off in the car. First, he took her to Matauri Bay, a gorgeous beach on the east coast. They had a long walk along the sand from one end of the beach to the other, while he told her about their first Christmas together, and how they'd hired a beach house and spent Christmas Day either in the sea or in bed. Phoebe listened and smiled, but inside felt wistful at the thought of all those early memories she'd lost. She wished she could remember for Rafe, because he spoke so lovingly of their early days. But just wishing wasn't going to make it so.

Afterward, he drove up to Mangonui, a quaint little fishing village at the edge of Doubtless Bay. They had a slow walk along the waterfront, then stopped at a chocolate shop called Treats to Tempt You and had a latte and a selection of their truffles.

"These are amazing," Phoebe said, sucking on a lemon creme as they walked back to the car.

"We come here all the time." Rafe took a kiwifruit truffle and popped it in his mouth. "We usually have a box of their chocolates at home, and we have dinner at Aqua Blue around once a month. And that's where we went for our cooking lessons." He gestured to the restaurant a few doors down from the chocolate shop, then glanced at her. "Ring any bells?"

Phoebe looked away, across the harbor to where the fishing boats were heading out to sea. The sunlight danced on the water, dazzling her. For a moment, she thought an image was forming, like seeing something out of the corner of her eye. But as she tried to grasp it, it slipped away, leaving her with a vague headache and a heavy feeling on her chest.

"Hey. I'm sorry, I shouldn't have asked." Rafe put his arm around her. "Come on, it's time we headed back."

"I'm okay. I don't want to go home yet."

He drove back toward Kerikeri and took her to Rainbow Falls. They stopped at the cafe outside and had some lunch, then walked along the path through the bush, hearing the rushing water through the palms and ferns. And then it appeared, the water tumbling over the rocks and falling nearly ninety feet into the deep green river.

"We came here on one of our first dates," Rafe said. "And it's also where I proposed to you."

Phoebe's eyes widened. "Oh my God, really?"

He took out his phone, tapped on the screen a few times, then turned it around to show her a photo he'd taken of her in this very spot. She was wearing her engagement ring and laughing, and there were tears on her cheeks.

She took the phone and stared at it, biting her lip. "I don't remember," she whispered. "I wish I did, but I don't."

"It's okay."

"It's not okay, Rafe. It's awful. I can't imagine how you must feel."

"I don't care," he said fiercely, pulling her into his arms. "All that matters to me is that you're here now. I don't care about the past."

It was a sweet thing to say, but she couldn't believe he meant it. She buried her face in his jacket, cursing the fact that she'd gone out of the house to run that evening. She never wanted to run again, never wanted to be reminded of that awful moment.

"It's going to be all right," he murmured, his arms tight around her. "We'll get through this, and one day we'll tell our kids about it, and we'll laugh at how weird these early days were. I know it feels bizarre now, but we're making new memories together, and that's what's important."

His jacket smelled of his body spray, warm and comforting. She listened to the water crashing down behind her, thinking about the photo. She'd looked so happy. How amazing it would have felt to have been dating this guy and then have him go down on one knee and ask her to marry him. She squeezed her eyes tightly shut, determined not to cry. It was pointless to get upset about it. As he said, they were making new memories and she had to concentrate on those and on what she had, not what she'd lost.

They stayed there like that for a while, as other visitors to the site passed quietly by them, casting small smiles. Then eventually, Rafe led her back to the car and drove home.

They walked inside, and Phoebe put her purse on the table and went over to the window, looking down at the river. Rafe came up behind her and put his hands on her upper arms. "Are you okay?"

"I feel a bit low. I'm sorry."

"No need to apologize. After what you've been through, I would think it's perfectly normal."

"I'm tired, that's all."

"We've done a lot today. Why don't you have a rest before we go out this evening?"

She hesitated, on the edge of tears, not wanting to leave him. She felt that if she were to sit down and really think, she'd be able to sort everything out, but her brain just wouldn't work the way she wanted it to.

"Come on," he said gently.

He led her into the bedroom, and when she got onto the bed, he stretched out beside her, fully clothed and on top of the covers. She snuggled up against him, and he kissed her forehead.

"I can hear the wheels spinning," he said, stroking her hair. "Just rest, sweetheart."

"I'm missing something," she mumbled. "It's right there, on the fringes, but I can't find it."

"You just need time."

She didn't want to sleep, she wanted to remember. But sleep came anyway, and everything faded to black.

*

"It's so good to see you," Dominic said. "You look so much better than when you first woke up."

They were sitting outside Marlin's Bar, at a group of tables on the corner of two of the main roads through Kerikeri. It was a balmy evening, and they were all wearing shorts and T-shirts. Despite her medication, Phoebe had requested a glass of wine, feeling the need to relax. Rafe had given in under protestation when she'd said she needed some Dutch courage to face everyone.

She'd been pleased to discover that the group meeting at Marlin's that evening included her brothers. Elliot was there with his girlfriend, Karen, and Dominic had brought his daughter, Emily. Libby was there with Mike, and several of their other friends. Rafe had introduced her, and everyone had been pleased to see her. She'd smiled a lot but hadn't said much, and had been relieved that they hadn't asked her too many questions. Had Rafe prepped them on that? She was thankful if he had.

She smiled at her eldest brother. The others were discussing rugby, Rafe leading the conversation as he talked about the lineup for the upcoming game against the Aussies. She hadn't had a chance to talk to Dominic alone yet. She adored the way he had his arm slung around his daughter, who'd curled up at his side. Emily was the spitting image of her mother, Jo, with long brown hair, a snub nose, and kind eyes.

"I feel better," Phoebe said. "It was lovely, though, waking up and seeing you there."

He smiled back. "I was so relieved when I looked up and saw you watching me."

"Have you really lost all your memories?" Emily asked.

"Not all of them," Phoebe said. "But I don't remember much about the last eight years."

"So, you don't remember me?" The girl didn't look upset, just curious.

"No," Phoebe said gently. "But I'll have fun getting to know you all over again."

Dominic's lips curved up. "She's very fond of her Auntie Phoebe."

Phoebe suspected he relied on his sisters for advice about bringing up a daughter. How awful for him to have lost his wife. She hesitated, wondering whether to mention it in front of Emily, then decided it was better to talk about the girl's mother than to act as if she'd never existed. "I just want to say, I'm so sorry to hear about Jo. That must have been such a difficult time for you both. She was lovely, and I'm going to miss her a lot."

"It was tough," he said, kissing the top of his daughter's head. "But we're doing okay, aren't we?"

Emily nodded. "Dad says Mum's wearing wings now, but they're plastic ones because she was allergic to feathers."

Dominic chuckled, and Phoebe smiled. She gave him an impish look. "So… am I supposed to call you the Reverend Dominic now?"

"Yep. And genuflect when you walk by me."

She grinned. "Seriously, though, I supposed I'm not really surprised when I think about it. You've always been a pillar of the community." He'd been one of the good guys at school, never getting into trouble and always receiving top grades, unlike Elliot, who'd constantly ended up in the Deans' office. Which was even funnier now he'd ended up as a cop.

Dominic smiled. "Jo helped make me the best version of myself I could be."

Phoebe met his eyes, seeing the sadness buried deep within them. He was far from over losing his wife, she thought, but he was doing the best he could for his daughter.

"If I swear in front of you do I have to say ten Hail Marys or something?" she asked him lightly.

"Well, that's Catholic and I'm Anglican, but yeah, something like that."

She chuckled. "Rafe said you're marrying us?"

"Yep. It was the first thing you asked me after you told me you were engaged."

She glanced across at Rafe. He was listening to Elliot talk about the recent All Blacks game against the Lions, the two of them bickering amicably about who they considered the man of the match. He sat back in his seat, long legs stretched out. He needed a shave, and the T-shirt he was wearing must have been five years old. His shorts were faded, his Converses scuffed. He was the epitome of casual scruffy sexiness.

"Some things don't change," Dominic said softly.

"What do you mean?"

"You still look at him as if he's the only guy in the world."

Her face warmed. "Aw," Emily said. "You're blushing."

"You think I'm doing the right thing going ahead with the wedding?" Phoebe whispered to them.

"You're like a prince and princess," Emily said. "You've got to get married."

"She's a big fan of the royal wedding," Dominic said. "And she has a point." He tipped his head to the side. "Are you having doubts, then?"

"I don't remember him, Dom. I wasn't sure if it was fair to marry him without any memory of what we'd had. I wasn't sure if I'd feel the same way about him. I seem to have changed so much over the past few years—what if the new me feels differently?"

"You don't look as if you feel differently."

"He's gorgeous," she said. "And he's charismatic. When he's around, I can't even think about anything or anyone else. But... sometimes I feel as if he's hiding something. Or maybe it's just my unease at not being able to remember. I'm not sure."

Dominic looked away, across the street, and for a brief moment Phoebe had the feeling that he knew exactly what Rafe was hiding from her. Did everyone know? Was there some big conspiracy going on?

Then he said, "Rafe loves you. You ought to hold on to that. You nearly died, Phoebe. It's amazing how quickly things can slip away from you."

He was thinking about his wife, that was all. One day, Jo had been there, and the next, she'd gone. Phoebe couldn't imagine how terrible that had been for him. He must have huge sympathy for Rafe, who'd nearly gone through the exact same thing. Of *course* he would recommend that they grab on to any hope of a happy future. She felt ashamed that she'd questioned it when he'd lost the one person he was supposed to be with.

She glanced back at Rafe, her heart giving a little jump when she saw him watching her. He wasn't smiling, and she wondered if he'd heard her question whether they should get married. His lips curved up then, though, and he winked at her.

Rafe loves you. You ought to hold on to that.

She was going to, with both hands.

Chapter Seventeen

"You were quiet this evening." Rafe turned the car onto the main road and headed for the bypass. "Are you feeling okay?"

"I feel fine. It was nice just to listen. I enjoyed that; thank you for taking me."

Rafe cast her a wry smile. "You're welcome. And you don't have to thank me."

"I don't have to be polite now we're getting married?"

"Are you teasing me?"

She smiled. "Maybe a bit."

"I can see you're almost back to your old self."

She looked out of the window. "I'm getting there."

He knew it was a half-truth. She hadn't recognized most of their friends, and seemed no closer to getting her memory back.

He'd assumed it would filter back gradually, like bringing a telescope slowly into focus, with small scenes popping into her mind one by one until the picture became clear. Maybe it wouldn't happen like that though; perhaps it would all come back to her in a big whoosh one day, and she'd be able to remember everything from the last eight years.

Or maybe it wouldn't come back at all.

Rafe had taken her to lots of places that held meaning for her, and she'd now met many of her friends and family. But nothing had worked.

She didn't speak for the remainder of the journey, and Rafe remained silent too, not sure how to comfort her. He pulled onto the drive and parked, and they got out and went inside. It was dark now, and the house was filled with shadows, a little stuffy and humid. She went into the bedroom, and Rafe followed, opening up the windows to let some air in. He went to turn on the light, but she reached out and stopped him.

He lowered his hand, frowning. "What's the matter?"

"Nothing."

Rafe reached out a hand and cupped her face. "Talk to me."

She moistened her lips with the tip of her tongue. He felt an answering twitch in his shorts, but ignored it.

"Take me to bed," she whispered.

His heart began to thud harder. Last night had been agony, forcing himself to keep his hands off her. "Phoebe…"

She stepped closer to him, tugged up his T-shirt, and slid her hands onto his skin. "I haven't touched you yet," she murmured, "or seen you naked. Why should you get all the fun?"

He caught her hands and removed them, giving her an exasperated look. "All in good time, sweetheart."

"Rafe, don't turn me down again. Please."

"I'm not having sex with you." He pushed her away as gently as he could. "You're not well, and it wouldn't be right."

"Fuck being right." Heat flared in her eyes.

His stomach flipped. Since her father had died, she'd become much more serious and focused. In the bedroom, though, she'd remained feisty, wanting to make love most nights, more than a match for his own high sex drive. Bearing in mind the doctor's speech to him in the hospital about changes to her libido, amongst other things, he'd been hesitant to think the previous night was a return to their old ways, but the look in her eyes now told him the old Phoebe was still there, and still wanted him as much as she'd always done.

Which was great, except he couldn't take advantage of that, not now. She wasn't in her right mind, and he had to step up and take care of her.

Not that she wanted taking caring of, by the looks of it.

She gave him a sultry look, running a finger down his chest, and he felt a flicker of warning. "I was okay yesterday, wasn't I?" she said sweetly. "I can't stop thinking about it, about you. I want to make love with you. I need to. Being with you, being close to you, doing the things we used to do… it might help my memory come back."

"I can't," he said, somewhat helplessly, "I'd never forgive myself if I hurt you."

"Jesus, you won't hurt me. You're the gentlest guy I know."

"Not in bed, I'm not."

Her eyes widened, sparking with excitement. Shit, that had been the wrong thing to say.

He ran a hand through his hair. "You make me lose my mind. I forget myself, and I can't afford to, not when you're like this."

"Just keep away from my head and we'll be fine." A smile danced on her lips.

"Don't joke about it," he snapped. "You nearly died. That was barely a week ago. Do you really think I can take you to bed and make love to you with that still in my head?"

Unperturbed as always by his temper, she moved closer to him again, trapping him against the bed. "You touched me yesterday. Pleasured me. Nothing terrible happened."

He put his hands on her arms, but couldn't bring himself to push her away. "It's not the same."

"The world didn't end, Rafe. I just want to touch you." She pulled up his T-shirt again and slid her hands underneath. "God, you feel good."

He shuddered and caught her hands by the wrists. "You've got to stop."

"I can't. I'm burning up." She did indeed look feverish, with flushed cheeks and glazed eyes. He knew that look, and knew that she'd already be swollen and wet, more than ready for him.

"Let's get in bed, then," he conceded desperately, "and do what we did yesterday."

"I don't just want an orgasm, Rafe. I want you inside me." She slipped out of his grasp and slid her hands up, her fingers reaching his flat nipples, and she rubbed her thumbs across them. It was like she'd put a taser to them, electric shocks of desire shooting through him.

"Jesus, fuck." He yanked her hands away.

"I know you want me." She pressed her hips to his, rubbing against his eager erection. "Don't you want to make love to me?" She pouted.

The pout reminded him that she was acting, instinctively doing what she'd done since they met, working him, knowing exactly what to do to turn him on. "You know I do," he told her, "but I'm not going to. Don't make this even more difficult than it already is."

Her jaw dropped as she realized he really was turning her down again. Her face reddened, and then her eyes blazed. "I can't believe you. What gives you the right to make this decision?" She tried to tug her wrists away from his grip, but he held on.

"I'm doing what's best for us both," he said firmly.

"Fuck you." Furious tears pricked her eyes as she fought with him.

"Phoebe, calm down, for God's sake. You're just upset…"

"Of course I'm upset! My fiancé won't have sex with me!"

"This isn't about me—"

"Let go of me!" She managed to yank one wrist free, but he still refused to let go of the other one. Outraged, she drew back her hand and slapped him around the face.

He saw stars for a moment. "Ouch," he said flatly. Now he was angry. He was trying to do what was best for her. He growled and tried to grab her arm.

She pushed him, hard. He stumbled back, met the bed, and fell onto the mattress.

Phoebe fell forward on top of him. She sat astride him and, when he caught her hands again, she used her weight to pin them above his head and kissed him, delving her tongue into his mouth.

He groaned, for a brief moment letting her, his body aching for her, then fought with her, heaving up and lifting her off him. She sank one hand into his hair though and gripped it tight, hooked a leg around his hips, and tugged him off balance. He fell heavily onto her, almost squashing her in the process.

He was going to have trouble now if he wasn't careful. Whether it was the medication or the wine or the sultry night or just whatever magic existed between them, her world had spun off balance, and she had the bit between her teeth. It didn't matter that she had no memory of ever sleeping with him—something within her knew what to do, and how to fire him up.

Pulling his head down to hers, she kissed him hungrily. Irritable that she knew how to turn him on, he tried to pull her hand free, but she refused to let go of his hair.

"Stop it," he snapped, lifting his head, and trying to push her leg away from his hips.

In reply, she slid her free hand down and flipped open the top button of his shorts.

He grabbed her hand. "Phoebe! You're driving me fucking insane."

She wrestled her hand free. "That's the plan." She yanked down the zipper and cupped his erection. "Holy shit. You're huge. Oh my God, I want that in me."

"Jesus." He knocked her hand away and tried to rear up, but she still had hold of his hair. Shifting on the bed, she caught him off balance, and he fell onto one elbow, trying not to hurt her. Their hips met, his erection nestling neatly against her mound.

Phoebe moaned and rocked her hips, arousing herself against him. She slipped her free hand beneath his T-shirt, then scored her nails down his back.

Rafe lost his temper. "Let go of my fucking hair," he yelled.

In reply, she pulled his head down to hers and bit his bottom lip.

"Ow!" He let out a string of swear words, his hands curling into fists. "What is it with you? Do you really want me to fuck you and just forget about the fact that you nearly died last week?"

She stared at him then, and stopped moving. Tears glimmered on her lashes. "I need you, Rafe," she whispered. "Please."

His anger died away. Wasn't that what he'd wanted all along?

Keeping his eyes on hers, he pulled up her dress, pushed down his shorts and boxers to free himself, and moved between her thighs. Tugging her panties to one side, he pressed the tip of his erection into her folds. She tilted up her hips, forcing him to slide a fraction inside her. He froze, groaned, and then pushed forward, going up to the hilt in one swift move.

She let out a long moan. "Oh holy Jesus, that feels good."

She was hot and wet and tight around him, and he'd missed her so much, missed being inside her, and felt spirited away into pleasure. "Is this better?" he murmured, pushing her thighs wide and filling the air with the slick sound of him moving inside her. "I wanted… to wait and… make it good for you." His voice caught with emotion, even as he thrust. "But you make me… lose my… mind…"

"I'm sorry," she whispered. "I couldn't wait."

He sighed, bent his head, and kissed her, moving his mouth slowly across hers, dipping his tongue inside, and she returned it with a moan of pleasure, running her other hand over his skin.

When he finally moved back, he whispered, "Let go of my hair."

She moistened her lips, and shook her head.

"Phoebe…"

"You might stop," she said, "so I'm not letting you go."

"I won't stop. I promise."

"I don't care." She tightened her fingers.

He winced. "Ouch." But he swelled inside her, and she moaned.

Sighing, he began to move again, long, slow strokes that she met with a rock of her hips, until it was as if they were engaged in a beautiful dance, moving perfectly in time with each other.

God, it felt so good, and he could feel her orgasm approaching, her breathing turning ragged. He kept a tight hold on his own desire, though, trying to stay in control so he didn't hurt her.

Clearly, Phoebe didn't want him in control. "More," she whispered. "Sweetheart…"

"Rafe, ah Jesus, I'm going to come… harder…"

Muttering under his breath about sirens leading him astray, he lifted onto his hands, grabbed a pillow, and slid it under her head to cushion the wound. She laughed at that and kissed him, wrapping her legs around his waist, and he gave in and started to thrust properly. Phoebe moved with him, crying out with pleasure, and she smelled so good, her sighs and moans filling his ears, her tongue in his mouth, and then she was coming so hard, so hard… strong pulses, clamping around him again and again. Her nails dug into his muscles, and he said her name over and over, his hips jerking as he spilled inside her. The room was hot, they were both sweaty, and he could taste salt and smell sex and feel wet and warmth and her soft, soft skin… She shuddered with little pleasurable aftershocks, and it was *ohhh*… fucking amazing…

"Holy shit, Phoebe." He gasped, his chest heaving. "What the hell do you do to me?"

She squirmed beneath him, clenching her internal muscles.

"Ow!" He groaned and hung his head, exhausted. "Please, please let go of my hair."

Finally, she released the short strands, lifting her arms above her head and stretching with a purr of pleasure. "Mmm."

He sighed. "Are you all right? Is your head okay?"

"What head?"

He gave a short laugh and withdrew, making her sigh. Lifting to one side, he then collapsed onto the bed on his back and closed his eyes.

She rolled onto her side facing him, sliding a hand down his chest to his groin and giving his still-firm erection a stroke. "You're all sticky," she said. "Yum."

"Will you stop? Are you trying to kill me?" He pushed her hand away. "You're insatiable, woman."

"It's my poor, damaged brain," she murmured.

"It's not your brain. You're always like this."

"Am I?" She sounded surprised.

He opened one eye and looked at her. "Always," he said. "It's why I love you."

She sucked her bottom lip. "Is it always like that?" she asked.

He sighed as the breeze from the open doors wafted over them. "Well, usually there's a lot more foreplay. And you don't pull my hair out by its roots." He rubbed the top of his head.

"Sorry," she said. "I didn't want you to stop."

"I wasn't going to."

"I didn't know that. I wasn't going to risk it."

He blew out a long breath. "I was only trying to do the right thing."

"I didn't want to do the right thing."

"I gathered."

"I like sex."

That made him laugh. "Me too."

"So we're always pretty… you know… steamy?"

"That was mild by comparison."

Her eyes widened. "Seriously."

"Girl, normally I'd have fucked you into next week and banged your head against the headboard. That was me being gentle."

"Holy moly."

"I told you. You do something to me."

She shivered. "I needed that, Rafe."

He turned his head to look at her. "Do you feel better now?"

"Much."

He met her gaze for a long moment.

Her smile faded, and she gave a little shake of her head.

He rolled his head back and looked up the ceiling.

Her memories weren't coming back. If making love like that wasn't going to trigger them, he couldn't imagine what would.

Chapter Eighteen

Phoebe parked her car down from the bridal shop and turned off the engine. Then she sat there for a moment, gathering her thoughts.

For the first time since she'd come out of hospital, she felt as if she was getting back to normal. Being with Rafe for four days had been amazing, but she was sure that returning to her everyday routine would finally eliminate the feeling of living in a science fiction novel that continued to plague her.

She missed Rafe already, though. She'd heard him rise and shower at seven a.m., but had been too sleepy to rouse while he dressed. He'd kissed her on the forehead before he left for his shift at eight, but hadn't attempted to wake her.

She was kind of glad he hadn't, a little embarrassed by what had taken place the night before. Now the fever had died down, she felt puzzled by how she'd acted. She would've assumed it was brought on by the brain injury, but he'd implied she was always like that. She thought about the way he'd fought with her, and how it had felt to have him sliding inside her, his muscles bunching and flexing beneath her fingertips as he thrust. Her body stirred, and she shifted uncomfortably. She'd watched him at the bar that evening, talking with his friends, and had been mesmerized by his husky chuckle, his wry sense of humor, the stubble on his jaw, his casual sexiness. No, maybe she wasn't surprised by her behavior. She had a feeling she was always going to superheat whenever Rafe Masters walked into the room.

But it was an odd relief to be on her own for once, and to be free of his presence. She'd enjoyed the drive into town, and she was looking forward to finding out a little of her old life that didn't involve him.

She got out of the car and locked it, crossed the road, and opened the door of the bridal shop. It gave a little jingle as she entered, and she stopped as the door swung shut behind her.

Once again, she was struck by the sensation of light and beauty as the sun streamed in across the white and cream gowns, bouncing off sequins and beads, dazzling her a little.

"Phoebe!" Her mother came out of the dressing rooms and walked toward her, holding out her hands in welcome. "Sweetheart. How are you?"

"I'm good, thanks. Feeling better every day."

"You look much better." Noelle searched her face as if she was peering through Phoebe's eyes into the dusty attics of her brain. "Any sign of the memory coming back?"

Phoebe pressed her lips together and shook her head. "Not yet."

"Oh well. Plenty of time. It's only been a week. Rafe gone back to work?"

"Yes, he's on days today and tomorrow."

"How have things been?" Phoebe blushed, and Noelle's gaze turned wry. "Like that, is it? Well, that doesn't surprise me. You always were like a couple of rabbits."

"Mum!"

"I thought he might have waited a bit longer. I guess he couldn't keep his hands off you."

"No," Phoebe muttered, deciding not to point out to her mother that it had been the other way around. "Anyway… I thought I might spend some time in the workroom familiarizing myself."

"Of course…" Noelle hesitated.

"What is it?"

"I just wondered… Is it worth you doing that if you're going to be leaving soon?"

Phoebe blinked. She'd completely forgotten about her impending move to Auckland. "Well, that's not for a few weeks yet, is it? I'd like to know more about the shop and how we set it up."

"Of course. Oh, by the way, I have something I want to show you. I didn't want to do it while Rafe was here, obviously." She beckoned for Phoebe to follow her, and they went into the changing rooms, and then through to a large office where Noelle obviously hung out when she wasn't serving. She closed the door, revealing an item hanging on the back.

Phoebe's jaw dropped. "Is that…"

"Your wedding dress." Noelle's eyes shone. "Want to see it?"

Swallowing hard, Phoebe nodded, and Noelle unzipped the plastic cover and removed it.

Phoebe stared in awe at the beautiful gown. It was full length alabaster satin, off-the-shoulder, and covered with a layer of the most exquisite lace she'd ever seen, each part of the pattern highlighted with tiny shining pearls.

"Did we make this?" she asked, coming forward to examine it.

"Of course. You and Bianca have spent hours on it."

Phoebe bit her lip. "It's gorgeous. But… I don't know if I'll ever get to wear it." The night before had been fun, but that didn't mean she was ready to commit to Rafe for life.

Noelle covered the gown with the plastic again. "There's still time, sweetheart. I've kept an eye on most of the organization, and let everyone know the situation. You wanted a small-scale wedding, so it's not as if there are thousands of people and millions of dollars involved. All the companies have said they are willing to wait until a day or two before to confirm whether it's going ahead, and most people who've been invited are keeping the day free." She rubbed her daughter's arm. "Anyway, have you had breakfast?"

"Um… no."

"Well look, why don't I get Bianca out of the workroom and we'll have a coffee and a muffin together with Roberta?"

"Okay."

Phoebe waited a little nervously while Noelle found Bianca. It was clear that her relationship with her twin had changed over the last eight years. Since coming out of hospital, she'd texted Bianca most days— sometimes Bianca had replied, sometimes not. It was nothing like when they'd communicated almost constantly. Of course, maybe it was just due to growing up and having lives of their own, but even so… Again, Phoebe had a niggly feeling deep inside that something was wrong, but she couldn't have said why.

But Bianca emerged with a huge smile, and came over and hugged her, and Phoebe pushed away her doubt, thinking that her lack of memory was making her paranoid.

"You look amazing," Bianca said, stepping back to admire her sister. "So much better than when you first came in."

"I think Rafe's been supplying his own medicine," Noelle said with a grin, leading her daughters through to the cafe.

"Ha!" Bianca rolled her eyes. "Didn't take you long to get back to normal, then."

"Does everyone know more about my love life than me?" Phoebe complained as they stepped down onto the cream tiles of the cafe.

"Difficult not to," Bianca said. "When we all went away in a beach house last summer, you two were so loud I had to wear earplugs."

"Oh Jesus."

Roberta laughed as she overheard the conversation and came forward to hug her sister. "Take no notice," she said, kissing her on the cheek. "It's wonderful to see you looking better."

"Lattes all around please," Noelle said, "and muffins, too. She needs to keep her strength up."

"The steaks will help with that," Phoebe said impishly, wanting to see their reactions. Sure enough, they all stared at her, startled. "I forgot I was a vegetarian," she said.

"Well." Noelle cleared her throat. "I suppose the protein is good for the brain at the moment."

"That's my excuse for eating bacon, and I'm sticking to it."

Laughing, they all took a seat at a table, and Roberta started making the coffee. Noelle went over to help with the muffins.

"So…" Bianca took her sister's hand. "You're feeling better."

"I am. I wondered if I could come with you to the workroom for a while today?"

"Of course!" Bianca beamed at her. "I'd love that."

"And I want you to tell me all about setting up the Bay of Islands Brides. It looks so amazing. I need to know the whole story."

"I suppose you don't remember anything," Bianca said.

"Not a thing," Phoebe said cheerfully. She watched her sister exchange a glance with her mother at the counter. Unease fluttered inside her again. She was imagining it, wasn't she? They weren't really hiding anything from her. "Rafe told me about our university course," she said, determined to ignore it. "We obviously did really well."

"We had a great time." Bianca accepted a muffin from their mother. "It was clear by our second year that we were going to do something related to weddings. We both loved wedding dresses. I loved the shape of them, designing the fit and flare, playing with sleek lines and meringues. You adored the intricate work, the beading, and the embroidery. We talked about making our own gowns all through our third year, and then we won the World of Wearable Arts award for our elven gown, and I think then we knew we definitely wanted to make more dresses."

"You used to talk about it a lot to me and your father," Noelle said, bringing over the remaining muffins and taking a seat. "Originally, you were just going to design individual dresses and sell them, but I'd always fancied running a shop. We had some money put away, and your father said what's the point in having it in the bank when it could be doing some good? There are no pockets in a shroud." She stopped and met Phoebe's eyes. As always when Phoebe thought about her father, she felt a twist inside and a flare of incredulousness that he wasn't there anymore. "Sorry," Noelle said, obviously seeing it on her face.

"It's okay. It still surprises me when I think he's not here. I guess we all took it pretty hard."

Again, Bianca and Noelle exchanged a look. She wasn't imagining it.

"Yes," Noelle said. "It was difficult for everyone."

Phoebe watched Roberta bring their tray of coffees over and distribute them. It was still early, and the shop was quiet, so she sat with them for a moment, and they all sipped their drinks.

"I have to ask you," Phoebe said quietly. "Is there something I should know? Something you're not telling me? I keep getting the feeling that I'm missing something, but I don't know what it is."

Noelle took a muffin and broke it in half on her plate. "Not that I know of, sweetheart."

"It's just difficult for us too," Roberta said. "A lot has changed, and it's funny to think you don't remember any of it."

"Like what?"

"Like Dad dying. And what happened to you after that."

"You mean how I took up running and that sort of thing?"

"You changed a lot," Bianca said. "You were like a different person, sometimes."

Phoebe sipped her coffee and then had a mouthful of muffin. They were tiptoeing around her, she could feel it. "Something tells me you didn't like that Phoebe much," she joked.

"Rubbish," Noelle scoffed. "It was bound to happen sooner or later, one or more of you moving on with your own lives. We've been very close for a long time, and it was a bit of a shock, that's all, when you announced you were moving away."

The muffin was lovely and moist, full of peaches and cream cheese, but Phoebe's appetite had disappeared, and she leaned back in her chair. She picked up a few crumbs with her finger and licked them off. "I don't know what to say to you about that. Obviously, Rafe got his promotion, and I suppose I had to go with him."

"Of course you did," Noelle said. "He's your whole world, and that's how it should be."

Phoebe glanced at Roberta, who smiled, and Bianca, who was looking into her coffee cup. "Do you… like him?"

Bianca looked up, and they all looked surprised. "Of course," Bianca said, but a touch of color appeared in her cheeks.

Phoebe frowned. "I just wondered if that's what was wrong…"

"We love Rafe," Roberta said, "and he's just perfect for you. He's taking you away from us, that's all. We built the shop together, and we're sad that you're going, but we want you to be happy."

But Bianca looked back at her cup and stirred the coffee with her spoon.

Phoebe didn't say anything else, forcing herself to eat a few more mouthfuls of muffin as the others discussed stock coming in that morning, and what they had planned for the day. But she kept thinking about that flush in Bianca's cheeks. Did she like Rafe in *that* way? Or was it the opposite—did she hate him for breaking the relationship with her twin sister?

The door jangled, and a couple of young women came into the bridal shop, pausing in the doorway with reverent awe as they studied the line of gowns. Noelle finished off her coffee and rose, touched her daughter's hair fondly, then went off to serve them. Roberta stood too, and picked up the plates with crumbs to take them back to the kitchen.

"I suppose we should get to work," Bianca said.

"In a minute," Phoebe replied. "I just want to say… is there anything you want to tell me? Anything we need to sort out, the two of us?"

Bianca's expression softened. "No, of course not."

"You're sure? I feel… funny. Like there's something wrong. I miss you." Tears pricked Phoebe's eyes at the thought that her relationship with her twin had somehow soured.

"There's nothing wrong." Bianca closed her hands over her sister's. "You've pulled away from me the last few years, that's all. It makes perfect sense—you have Rafe, and I suppose I get jealous sometimes because he's gorgeous, and I don't have anyone of my own yet. And now you're moving away… The thing is, I love the shop, and we had so many plans." She bit her lip. "I admit that sometimes I feel resentful and angry toward Rafe because of that. But it's only fleeting. Roberta's right—we do want you to be happy."

Phoebe tried to blink her tears away. "I don't know that I want to go now," she whispered. "But I don't want to disappoint Rafe. If it's really what he wants, and he can't get promotion here because the station's too small…"

"Oh God, you have to go with him, I understand. I'm just sad, that's all."

Phoebe was sad too, and a tad resentful. Why was it she who had to give up her dream for Rafe? Why wasn't he content staying in Kerikeri? They had a home and a busy social life. He'd said he wasn't ambitious, but he obviously was or else he wouldn't be throwing away what they had because the grass was greener on the other side.

"Don't be blue," Bianca said. "Come on, let's go in the workroom. That always cheers you up."

Phoebe let her sister lead her through the bridal shop and out the back into the workroom. It was only now that she realized they'd built a viewing platform at the top with a railing, so visitors could watch and talk to them while they were sewing. Bianca opened the gate and closed it behind them, and they descended into the workroom.

"I'll give you a tour," Bianca said.

Phoebe followed her around as her sister showed her where they kept the patterns, and the shelf of notebooks where they sketched their ideas. There were large folders of magazines with sticky notes highlighting dresses they liked, or bits of dresses—a neckline here, a hemline there, a ring around a particular piece of embroidery that Phoebe had liked. She recognized her own handwriting, but didn't remember writing any of the notes.

There were shelves of material, carefully wrapped to protect against dust and the strong sunlight, and Phoebe ran careful fingers over the rolls of satin, silk, and tulle in various shades of white and cream.

Then, eventually, she went over to the drawers of beads and buttons she'd spotted the other day. Bianca left her to it, and she pulled a stool up in front of the unit and started looking through the drawers. They were so beautiful, like little gemstones, all glittering and shining, and there were tiny shells too, and sequins, mini pearls, little round buttons, and thousands of different white and cream beads, some the size of a pin head, others as big as her thumbnail.

Her heart swelled, and tears pricked her eyes yet again. She loved it here. She felt so happy, and she knew she could easily sit there for hours day after day, playing with these beads and stitching them onto the dresses.

They'd obviously spent years getting to where they were right now. So why was she giving it all up for a man?

Of course it wasn't any man, it was Rafe, who set her alight with just a look, and to whom she'd obviously been devoted from the start. Instinctively, she knew she would have followed him wherever he asked, around the world if necessary.

But this was her dream, her life. Her family were here, and her friends. Was it right that he'd asked her to leave it all behind for him?

Chapter Nineteen

At just before six p.m., Phoebe pulled up in the car park next to the fire station. She'd spent the morning at the bridal shop, but around one p.m. had started flagging, and Noelle had sent her home. After a two-hour nap, she felt much better physically. Emotionally, though, her thoughts were still whirling. She wanted to talk to Rafe, and decided she'd catch him straight out of work and take him to dinner.

She rounded the building and stopped in surprise as she saw one of the fire trucks out the front. Clearly, it had just returned from a call, because the firefighters getting down from it were all in uniform, some of them covered in soot and sweat.

Until now, she hadn't given much thought to Rafe's career. She'd liked the idea that he did something important, and that he had a steady and stable job, but she'd assumed he'd fallen into it, rather than it being a role he'd dreamed about from his youth.

But as she watched the firefighters talking and laughing, she knew that this wasn't a job that someone could do without putting in a hundred percent. They had to be able to work as a team, and the physical nature of the job meant they had to be at the peak of fitness all the time.

Phoebe's breath caught in her throat as her gaze fell on Rafe, standing to one side and directing some of the others as they sorted out the equipment. He'd told her he was a senior firefighter, so maybe he'd been in charge of the firefighters on the call. He must have gone with them because he was in uniform, his helmet under his arm.

After finishing his conversation, he turned to walk into the fire station and then saw her. His eyebrows rose in surprise, and he immediately crossed the forecourt toward her.

"Hey," he said. "I wasn't expecting to see you here. Everything okay?"

Phoebe nodded. He looked huge in the thick jacket and trousers, and his blue eyes blazed in his soot-stained face. His hair was spiky with sweat.

He frowned and dipped his head to look her in the eye. "Are you feeling all right?"

The speech center of her brain was refusing to work. She just nodded again, her heart racing. Clearing her throat, she forced herself to say something. "I'm… um… fine. I thought I could take you out to dinner. I forgot that you might have been out on a call."

"That sounds great. Give me five minutes for a shower and I'll be with you."

She nodded. Mmm. The guy looked amazing. She could have pushed him onto the concrete and done him then and there.

He continued to frown at her, and then, like the clouds clearing in the sky, his frown lifted, and his lips curved up. "I can leave the uniform on if you like," he said silkily.

Her eyes widened. "Jesus. You're filthy and sweaty. That's the last thing I'd want."

"Yeah, right. I know what you're thinking. Your eyes have glazed over." He moved closer to her. "Give me a kiss."

"Rafe!" She shoved him away, and he laughed.

"All right. Five minutes." He walked away, sending her a last, hot look over his shoulder.

Mumbling under her breath, she walked back to her car. What was it about him that scrambled her brain whenever he was near? All thoughts except lewd ones fled her mind whenever he looked at her.

In the end, it was seven minutes before he joined her. His hair was damp, curling at the temples, and he smelled of warm, clean male, his body wash filling her nostrils with the scent of lemon and lime. He made her mouth water.

"Better than sweat and soot," he said, and she realized she'd said the words out loud.

"Much better," she agreed, although part of her wished he had kept the uniform on.

His eyes told her that he knew exactly what she was thinking, but he didn't tease her. He just smiled and said, "So where are we going?"

*

Phoebe had booked a table at the local Italian restaurant, and they walked there slowly, Rafe draping an arm around her shoulders.

"If you wanted to get in my boxers, you could have just said so," he murmured in her ear, smiling when she blushed.

"I just thought it would be nice to eat out," she said. That might have been so, but she was looking at him as if she wanted him for dinner, and Rafe couldn't stop his own thoughts turning to images of her last night, soft and willing beneath him.

She pushed his arm off her shoulders as they entered the restaurant. "Will you stop looking at me like that?"

"It's your fault."

"How's it my fault?"

He waited until they were seated at their table, and the waiter had handed them their menus and retreated. He liked this restaurant, and although Phoebe obviously didn't remember it, they ate there often, usually at this table, on the flagstones outside, lit by the rays of the evening sun, with the citronella candles keeping away the insects. The tables were wooden and covered with checked cloths, and the menu was simple, but everything was cooked fresh. The scent of garlic and herbs mingled with the sound of Vivaldi's *Four Seasons* playing in the background.

"You turned up at the station looking like a piece of summer in that dress," he said, "staring at me as if you were thinking about a reenactment of last night. You switched my brain to lust, and now it won't go back again."

She wore a long white beach dress that was completely transparent when the sun was behind her. He was betting she hadn't realized that. He'd tell her about it later.

She tore her gaze away to look at the list of dishes. "I did nothing of the sort. It's all in your imagination."

He chuckled. "If you say so."

"I think I'll have the fettuccine," she said.

"Steak for me. Gotta keep my strength up." He folded the menu shut, leaned on the table, and winked at her.

"You've changed your tune." She closed her menu and leaned back, obviously trying to put some distance between them. "Last night you were all, 'Don't touch me, Phoebe. I mustn't.'" Her eyes taunted him. She was flirting with him again, even if she didn't realize it. Jeez. The woman really was insatiable.

"I was trying to help," he said mildly.

"I was right though," she pointed out. "Everything went fine."

"Only because we were in missionary and I took it easy."

Her gaze dropped to his lips. "What would you have done normally?"

He opened his mouth to reply, but the waiter was approaching, so instead he smiled and gave his order, and Phoebe gave hers. They chose a soft drink each, and the waiter went to relay the order.

"You were saying," Phoebe said.

He gave her a wry look. "I think we should change the subject. Have you seen the weather report? Apparently, there's a cyclone on the way."

She pouted, but soon replaced it with a smile. "I thought it was getting windy earlier. We'll have to batten down the hatches."

"Yeah. How has your day been?"

"It was good. I spent until one o'clock in the shop, and even did some sewing."

"Oh, great. I'm glad."

"And I spent some time with mum and the girls." She sucked her bottom lip, giving him an appraising look. "Can I ask you something?"

His heart skipped a beat, but he forced a smile onto his lips. "Of course."

"Was there ever anything between you and Bianca?"

That took him completely by surprise. "No! Never."

"Don't lie to me, Rafe, it's not fair when I can't remember."

"I'm not lying." Her words shocked him. "I have no romantic feelings for Bianca, and she doesn't have any for me, as far as I'm aware. Why would you think that?"

She frowned and looked down, turning the pepper pot in her fingers. "It's like there's a riptide running beneath everything, and everyone else knows where it is except me. It keeps tugging at me, threatening to pull me under, then disappears just as I catch sight of it."

Rafe leaned back as the waiter delivered their drinks, and he took a minute to take a few sips of his soda. Noelle had texted him that morning, asking him to call her when he was on a break. He'd done so mid-morning, and she'd told him that Phoebe was starting to ask questions. Alarmed by this, Rafe had told Noelle that it was time they told Phoebe everything. For a start, it wasn't fair to keep secrets from her. And if she were to get her memory back, she wouldn't appreciate that they'd tried to keep her in the dark.

But Noelle had begged him to keep quiet a little longer, and he'd reluctantly agreed. Now, he wished he hadn't. It was clear that Phoebe was picking up on an undercurrent running through her family. She'd always been astute, and she must have been able to sense Bianca's resentment of their plans. He hated that she thought it might be due to jealousy of their relationship.

"I just wish I could remember," she whispered. "Everything, I mean. My father dying. And why it changed me so much. Why don't I feel that now? I have no urge to run or stop eating meat! And as for the shop…" She met his gaze for a moment, then looked away.

"What?" he said softly.

"I know you want promotion," she said. "And I want to support you all the way. But the shop's so amazing… I can't believe I'm giving it all up…" Her gaze came back to him, holding a touch of resentment.

Jesus, she blamed him.

For a moment, Rafe couldn't think what to say. The last thing he wanted was to be an ogre in her eyes, and it stung that she thought he was making her leave. But he didn't want to have that conversation now. Not in the restaurant, spilling the truth over the dinner table as sure as if he'd sliced a knife through his guts. Maybe later, maybe tomorrow. Not now.

"This was supposed to be a romantic dinner," he said, leaning forward again. "There's plenty of time to talk about the future. Why don't we concentrate on the here and now tonight?"

She surveyed him for a moment, and then gave a little smile and nodded. "All right," she said. "So, to return to our earlier conversation, you implied last night was tame by our standards. Describe to me a normal state of affairs in bed."

He gave a short laugh and turned his fork in his fingers. If talking about sex would keep her mind away from more serious matters, maybe he should give in. "Okay," he said. "Normally, we're very mobile. We change positions several times. So… I guess I'd have started on the bed like we did, then had you on top, then tossed you onto your front and fucked you from behind."

Her jaw dropped, and her eyes widened. "Holy shit."

He leaned back as the waiter brought over their rosemary bread, and waited for the guy to depart. "What?" he said, breaking off a piece of the bread and holding it out to her.

"You like to shock me," she scolded, dipping the bread in the little bowl of olive oil, then in the salt.

He did the same and winked at her. "Maybe."

She chewed the bread, eyeing him, and he could see the questions plaguing her like mosquitoes.

"Ask away," he said, dipping another piece of bread.

"We can't sit at the dinner table and talk about sex," she scolded.

"Of course we can. We're getting married next week. It's almost legal."

That made her laugh. "I don't know what to say. It makes me go all hot."

"You say that like it's a bad thing."

"I mean it makes me embarrassed."

"After last night? Why?"

"I don't know. It's as if that was another Phoebe, as if I'm possessed and she takes me over."

He smiled at her fondly. It must be hard for her, he thought. In her head, she was only eighteen, with none of the sexual experiences she'd had over the years. She couldn't remember the first guys she'd been with. He kind of liked that. But oddly, something within her obviously retained her sexual experiences, because she hadn't reacted to him like a virgin. In bed, she'd very much been his Phoebe, as sexy and energetic and lusty as always.

"So what would innocent Phoebe like to know?" he asked.

"I don't know… um… Have we ever had sex outdoors?"

He laughed. "Ah, yeah. A few times."

"Really?"

"Yep. On the beach, more than once. In the forest. And on the domain, behind a tree."

"Oh my God, seriously?"

"Dead serious."

"That must have been your idea," she said.

"That one was, yeah. We were walking home, and I was feeling horny. You didn't object though, I have to point out."

"You're very persuasive," she said. "I bet I only did it to please you."

"Yeah, you keep telling yourself that."

The waiter came to take away the plate, and they watched each other as he laid out the cutlery and refreshed their drinks.

"Tell me more," she said when the waiter had retreated again.

"Like what?"

Her eyes held a wistful longing. "I don't remember anything, Rafe, not our first time, or our last time, or anything in between. You have all these memories, like hundreds of photographs stored in an album I never get to see."

His heart went out to her, and he leaned on the table and took her hand in his. "Our first time was in the house I used to share with Elliot. He was out, under strict instructions not to return for a few hours."

"A sock on the door?"

"Pretty much. We made out on the sofa for a while, and then went into my room. You were shy to begin with, a bit nervous, and I think I must have been too, because I got my watch caught in your hair, and then my zipper got stuck… We started laughing, and then it just got better from there."

"How did we do it?" she whispered, leaning her chin on her hand.

"You on top, for a while. You were amazing." His gaze drifted into the distance as he remembered that moment when she'd climbed on top of him. Her skin had gleamed in the sunlight, her rosy nipples tightening in his fingers. He'd wanted to take it slowly, to make sure he didn't hurt her, but she'd lowered herself on top of him and he'd slid all the way in, and only seconds later they were moving together as if it was their hundredth time.

"Then I rolled you underneath," he said. "I tried to be all gentlemanly about it, and go slowly, but you said, 'Don't hold back, Rafe, I won't break.'"

She gave a short laugh. "I said that?"

"You did, so I didn't. I'm surprised the bed held up. Apparently, next door thought I was putting up a shelf because of all the banging."

Phoebe blushed. "Oh my God."

"Yeah. We've had a few complaints over the years, actually. Usually in hotels."

Their dinner arrived at that moment. Rafe watched her while the waiter placed their plates before them, and tried not to laugh at her scarlet face.

He waited until the waiter had left before he added, "Normally, I ask for a room at the end so the bed's not against a neighboring wall."

She twirled a fork in her fettuccine. "Now I know you're teasing me."

"I'm really not. We're very…" He stopped cutting into his steak and thought about it for a moment. "Enthusiastic," he chose, popping the piece of steak in his mouth.

She surveyed him as she ate, her eyes curious.

"I am," he said. "Telling the truth. I can't think of anything that two people can do on their own in the bedroom that we haven't done."

Her fork paused. "Even…"

"Even that."

She gave him a wry look. "You don't know what I was going to say."

"You were going to say anal sex."

She gasped and looked around to make sure nobody had overheard them. He laughed, captivated by this innocent, blushing Phoebe.

"I can't believe you said that out loud," she whispered.

He leaned forward, looked her in the eye, and mouthed the words clearly: "Anal. Sex."

She inhaled again, but her lips curved up and her eyes danced.

"Did you know that the word anus comes from the Latin, meaning ring?" He had a sip of his drink. "Puts a whole new perspective on the question of exchanging rings at the wedding ceremony."

"You're so wicked!" she scolded.

"I'm what you made me, sweetheart," he said. And he cut another piece of steak, guessing by the glitter in her eyes that he was going to need every ounce of iron and energy the meat could afford him that evening.

Chapter Twenty

Phoebe ate the rest of her dinner without tasting a single bite. Once again, Rafe had bewitched her with his incessant talk of sex and kissing and licking and God-knew-what-else, tempting her throughout the rest of the meal with tales of things they'd done and things he'd like to do.

Did he know what he was doing to her? She was pretty sure he did. Now they'd had sex and she'd not fallen into a coma, he appeared to think it was okay to tease her into a sexual stupor, and he also appeared to know exactly how to do it.

Phoebe would not have guessed that she liked a man to talk dirty to her, but she couldn't deny that the wicked things he whispered to her over her pasta sent her aquiver with yearning. When he told her about the first time he'd brought home a vibrator and tried it out on her, she felt a twinge between her thighs as her muscles contracted involuntarily. When he described—in great detail—about the time he'd first tied her down and spent an hour licking her from head to toe, she nearly came on the spot.

"Tell me you'll have sex with me tonight," she whispered as they shared a portion of Tiramisu.

He licked the coffee-and-chocolate dessert off the spoon in a way that made her shiver. "We'll see," he said.

She narrowed her eyes. He smirked.

"You're not in charge in this relationship," she told him.

He had another mouthful of Tiramisu. "We'll see," he repeated. "Want me to tie you down again?" He flicked his eyebrows up.

Ooh, this man was so sexy she could have eaten him for dessert instead of the Tiramisu. In fact… maybe she would. That was an idea.

He pursed his lips. "What's going through your mind?"

"Personal private thoughts," she said.

"So, something sexy then?"

"Maybe." She finished off the Tiramisu. She was so sexed up, she felt as if her hair was lifting around her head with static. "Come on, Masters. Finish your drink and let's get going."

He chuckled, and they paid and headed for the car park. "I'll meet you back home," he said, heading for his own car.

Phoebe drove the short distance to their house, barely remembering the drive, only just registering the increasing wind that buffeted the car as the cyclone clipped the New Zealand coast. Every cell in her body seemed focused on the guy in the car behind her. By the time they pulled up at the house, she was in a fog of desire, unable to think about anything except Rafe and all the things he'd said that evening.

He opened the front door, and Phoebe went in, then turned as he closed the door and pushed him up against it. Sliding her hands up his body and into his hair, she pulled his head down and kissed him.

Rafe sighed and kissed her back, resting his hands on her butt and pulling her to him so she could feel that he was aroused too. But after a minute he lifted his head and carefully removed her hands from his hair.

"Let's get in the door," he said. "I need a drink." He walked off into the kitchen.

Phoebe leaned on the doorjamb and watched him take a heavy-bottomed glass out of the cupboard, toss a few ice cubes in it, then pour over them a glug of pale yellow whisky. When he'd done, he turned and leaned against the counter, facing her, and took a large mouthful from the glass. He swallowed it and sighed, and she imagined that heat searing through him, the way it was through her without any alcohol at all.

They watched each other for a moment. Eventually, he gave a short laugh. "Am I going to make it out of here alive?"

She pushed off the doorjamb and walked into the room, coming to stand before him. "Do you want to?"

He tipped his head from side to side as if he was thinking about it, then smiled. "Come into the bedroom?"

Phoebe slid her hands beneath the hem of his T-shirt. All evening, he'd played her, using his knowledge of their sexual history to unsettle and shock her. It was time she took some of the control back.

"I want you naked," she said, pulling up the top.

"In the kitchen?" He put his glass down, lifted his arms, and let her remove the tee.

She dropped it to the floor and placed her hands on his bare chest. "Yes." It was the first time she'd done this, and she fanned out her hands and brushed them across his pecs. "You have hair."

"Most men do," he said, amused.

"You have an amazing body." She was breathless with admiration.

"Thank you."

"I mean it." She trailed her fingers down, over his defined abdominal muscles. "You look like a Greek god." Her fingers reached the button of his jeans, and she flicked it open.

He leaned his hands on the edge of the counter, not stopping her, although he looked a little wary, as if wondering what she had in mind.

Keeping her gaze on his, she slid down the zipper of his jeans carefully and pushed them down his legs. He toed off his Converses and stepped out of the jeans, and she kicked them away.

Then she dropped her gaze to his boxer-briefs. They fit snugly to his slim waist, muscular butt, and thighs. His erection strained against the black cotton, begging her to set it free.

Hooking her fingers in the elastic at the top, she pulled the underwear over his erection and down his thighs. Rafe let her, his eyelids lowering to half-mast as he stepped out of them.

Phoebe dropped the boxers on top of his jeans and stepped back to admire him. Mmm. Wow. Old Phoebe had really done a good job in picking the man she was going to marry. This guy was going to be hers, to have and to hold, for the rest of her life. She'd be waking up beside him every morning and going to bed next to him every night. She could make love with him all day, every day, if she wanted. She was the luckiest woman in the world.

She lifted her gaze to his. His lips had curved up.

"It's all yours," he said.

"Yum." She licked her lips, and he chuckled.

Leaning forward, she reached past him and picked up a small jar. He looked down as she unscrewed the top and raised an eyebrow. "Are you hungry?"

She shook her head, took a teaspoon out of the drawer, and dipped the tip into the jar of Nutella. Taking it out, she touched it to his nose. He gave her an exasperated look, and she giggled and leaned forward to lick it off.

"Have I done this before?" she asked him, dipping the spoon back in the jar.

"No," he murmured.

"Good." She took the spoon out and this time touched it to his lips. Automatically, he licked them, but she shook her head, then leaned forward to do it for him.

Ooh, he tasted good, and she brushed her tongue into his mouth, enjoying the slick slide of it, the heat that spread through her as he returned the kiss with enough passion to convince her that he was holding back, letting her proceed at her own pace.

She dipped the spoon again, and this time touched the back of it to each of his nipples. Rafe gave a patient sigh, and she smiled as she bent to lick the chocolate spread off, taking her time to trace the tip of her tongue around each nipple.

When she'd done, she moved back and stripped off her dress in one swift move. His eyes widened, but when he stepped forward she pushed him back against the counter, dropped to her knees, and picked up the jar again.

"Oh jeez," he said.

She moistened her lips with the tip of her tongue, scooped up a big spoonful of the spread, which had turned almost runny in the heat of the kitchen, and then held it over the top of his erection. It drizzled over his skin, running down the shaft.

"Are you trying to give me a yeast infection—*aaahhh!*" He inhaled sharply as she lowered her mouth over the end, brushing her tongue across the sensitive skin. Groaning, he dropped his head back, and she felt a surge of smug pleasure as she proceeded to lick off all the chocolate.

Ohhh... he tasted good, and she loved the way he swelled in her hand as she stroked him. She didn't remember doing this before, and yet somehow she knew what to do; she knew how to wrap her lips over her teeth, and that he liked her taking him as deep as she could, sucking hard.

She stroked and sucked, stroked and sucked, and even though she wanted him inside her, part of her wanted him to come in her mouth, to make him lose control. But just when she thought she was getting somewhere, he extricated himself carefully, and then slid his hands beneath her arms and lifted her.

"Hey," she grumbled. "I was enjoying that."

He shook his head. "What am I going to do with you?"

"What do you mean?"

He sighed and kissed her, turning to push her up against the counter, and as she lifted her arms around his neck she felt his hands behind her back, undoing her bra. He slid the straps down her arms and dropped it onto the floor, and her panties followed soon after. Now they were both naked, and her body warmed as he pressed his against it. It was the contrast she loved—he was all flat planes and hard surfaces and tanned skin, and she was smooth and curvy and pale.

"You're filling out," he said as if reading her mind, cupping her face. "The hollows have gone beneath your cheeks."

"You don't like me thin?" she whispered.

"I love you every way," he said, but something told her he was lying. He didn't like what she'd become, all her training, the physical demands she'd put on her body.

Bending, he kissed down her neck to her breasts and covered a nipple with his mouth, and she dropped her head back, sinking a hand into his hair. She'd been turned on all evening, but this fine-tuned her desire, teasing her a little more toward the edge with every lick and suck of her sensitive skin.

"Rafe," she whispered, aching for him, but in reply he just dropped to his knees the same way she'd done, pushed her legs apart, and sank his mouth into her.

She gasped at the sensation of his tongue sliding into her folds, shocked and excited at the same time. He lifted her leg over his shoulder, giving himself better access, and she felt him slide his fingers inside her, as his tongue continued to swirl over her clit.

Oh God, she wasn't going to last long like this. "Stop," she whispered, "I'm going to come," but he didn't, holding her tightly as he sucked on her clit, and she gave in and came, clamping around his fingers and crying out with each delightful pulse.

When she'd done, he withdrew his fingers and got to his feet. "I'm sorry," she said, disheveled and disappointed it was over so quickly. "I wanted it to last longer."

"That was just the *hors d'oeuvres*." He put his hands under her butt and lifted her onto the worktop. "This is the main course." He pushed her knees wide, tugged her to the edge, and guided the tip of his erection into her folds. Slowly, he slid inside her.

Phoebe closed her eyes and reveled in the sensation of being so close to him, so intimate. She could feel him all the way up, right to the top.

She opened her eyes as he began to move, and kept her gaze on his as he thrust. She was wet and swollen from her orgasm, super-sensitive, and the feeling of him sliding inside her was bliss.

"You feel good," he said, his voice husky, and he kissed her leisurely, taking his time to brush his tongue over her lips, to tease them with his teeth, and to stroke his tongue against hers.

"You too," she whispered back.

"Marry me," he murmured. It was the first time he'd asked her since she laid eyes on him at the hospital. He'd obviously decided to wait a while, but now, inside her, the two of them moving like clockwork, he couldn't hold back anymore. "Be my wife. Let me do this with you every night for the rest of our lives."

"Yes," she said. "I love you." She hadn't meant to say it, but she wasn't surprised when the words left her lips. It didn't matter that she couldn't recall their past. Her feelings for him hadn't changed. Somehow, her body remembered the love they'd shared, and she wasn't going to throw it away.

He stopped moving and cupped her face. He looked genuinely choked with emotion. "You're sure?"

She nodded and blinked away sudden tears. "Of course I am. I'm crazy about you, Rafe. Can't you tell? I want to spend the rest of my life getting to know you all over again."

A frown flickered on his brow, and he looked as if he was about to say something. But then he smiled, and he lowered his head and kissed her, the sweetest, most tender kiss she thought she'd probably ever had.

She swallowed hard. "Okay, enough being soppy." She met his gaze and lifted her chin. "Now fuck me. Hard as you like."

He raised his eyebrows and laughed. "Yeah, you've not changed." To her surprise, he withdrew, but before she could complain, he picked her up in his arms and carried her through to the bedroom.

"I like the kitchen," she grumbled.

"Me too, but you still have a head injury, and I want you to be comfortable when I screw you senseless." Laughing at the look on her face, he tossed her gently onto the bed. "Get on your front."

She wriggled up to the pillows and lay on her back. "No."

He climbed on the bed and rolled her over easily. She fought him, but in seconds he'd parted her legs, lowered on top of her, and slid inside her.

"*Aaahhh…*" She buried her face in the pillow.

"I'm going to make you come again now," he stated, sliding a hand beneath her and brushing a finger over her clit.

She moaned, pinned there by his weight, unable to do anything but lie there as he began to move, his hips meeting her butt with a smack every time he thrust. *Ohhh…* this way was animal and base and feral, and oh dear God he was so good at it. She thought she'd started in control, but now she realized it was only because he'd let her. Her body was his to command, and right now he was going to take his pleasure from her, and there was nothing she could do about it.

She came again, brought to the brink as much by the thought of him possessing her as by his physical touch, but still he thrust, and she opened her thighs wide and just let him, loving every minute, happy to be the object of his lust. His breathing turned ragged, and he lifted up and pressed her into the pillows with a hand on her back as he gave those final few thrusts, and she shuddered as he came, feeling him spurting inside her as he groaned.

One day they'd make a baby. Suddenly, she wanted it more than anything, the fierce desire taking her by surprise. There was nothing about this that wasn't physical and instinctive, born out of a natural urge to mate and procreate. Why were they waiting? She wanted to make a child with him, to bind him to her, so she'd always have a little piece of him to hold that she'd never lose.

He kissed her neck, her hair, the wound on the back of her head, her shoulders, her neck again, and then carefully withdrew and pulled her into his arms. Her thighs were wet, but she was too tired to do anything about it. He moved, though, leaning across to the bedside table, and she heard him take a tissue out of the box, then felt his hand between her thighs, mopping up the moisture before drying himself. He tossed the tissue aside, and she curled up against him.

"I want a baby," she whispered.

He went still. She lifted up and looked at him.

Tears glistened on his lashes. "I love you," he said.

"I love you, too." She lowered back down and rested her cheek on his shoulder.

Her thoughts wandered lazily, images looming in her mind and then fading away again, like colored balloons floating around in the sky. Night was falling, and she could hear a morepork—a native owl—hooting somewhere in the bush. Rafe was breathing evenly, and she thought he might have dozed off already. She smiled and closed her eyes.

It was only as sleep settled over her that she realized she'd still not gotten to the bottom of her earlier unease. Rafe had kept her distracted all evening, quite skillfully, she thought, by bringing every conversation back to sex as if he'd known that while she was hazy with desire, she couldn't concentrate on anything else.

She wanted to think about it more, but she was too tired, and she soon fell asleep.

*

Rafe felt Phoebe relax against him, and knew she'd finally dozed off.

I want a baby. Her words had almost made him cry. He wanted to laugh, to dance, to celebrate the fact that she wanted to marry him, to have a child with him, to spend the rest of her life with him.

But as he lay there in the darkness, looking up at the ceiling, his heart was heavy, and it was a long while before sleep claimed him.

Chapter Twenty-One

The next day, after Rafe had left for work, Phoebe made herself a coffee and sat at the desk in the living room overlooking the river.

The wind had increased overnight, and now it was raining, the brief gusts throwing the droplets at the glass in angry handfuls. The weather report had said the cyclone was going to hit hardest farther down the coast, but high winds would still trouble the Bay of Islands. Inside, though, it was cozy, warm, and comfortable.

She pulled the wedding box toward her.

Up until now, she'd steadfastly ignored the fact that they were supposed to be getting married on Tuesday. She'd assumed she'd end up cancelling it, and she expected that everyone else thought that would be the case, too. The days since the accident had passed in a whirl, and she knew her mother had tried to give her a bit of space to let her recover, and had dealt with some of the preparations herself.

But now it was time to sort everything out. It was Friday, just four days until the big day, and last night she'd told Rafe she was going to marry him.

Was it still possible? It seemed crazy to think they could go ahead so close to the date, although her mother had promised that she'd kept an eye on everything over the past few days.

Her fingers brushed across the folder as she thought about the night before. It was true that she continued to have a niggling feeling deep down that something was awry, but she was beginning to think it was some stray neuron in her brain that was interfering with her radar. There was no big secret, no unpleasant surprise waiting to spring on her. Rafe loved her—that much was clear, and everyone seemed happy for the two of them. She would gain nothing by cancelling the wedding, and would gain everything by going ahead.

She was going to do it—she was getting married!

Inhaling with a sudden burst of excitement and pleasure as she thought of the look on Rafe's face when she told him that evening that it was all going ahead, she opened the box. Rafe had told her that she hadn't wanted a wedding planner but had wanted to do it herself. Now she questioned the idiocy of that statement, but she'd always been organized in the past, and she was relieved to see she hadn't changed much as she took out the folders inside and began going through them.

She spent a couple of hours reading, making notes on a pad as she went. She'd obviously arranged everything not long after Rafe had asked her to marry him, and she must have rung the companies once a month to check on the progress, because she'd written down the date of each phone call and ticked it.

After she'd familiarized with the organization—the flowers, the venue, the cars, the photographer, the band, suit hire for Rafe and Elliot, his best man—she stopped and made herself another coffee and a plate of toast with peanut butter. Taking a bite and crunching it, she returned to the desk and made a list of all the companies she needed to call. Then she started ringing each of them in turn.

After an hour, she took a break, pleased that she'd contacted the major companies involved and everyone was fine with it going ahead. She sat by the window for a while, watching the wind whip the palm trees, thinking about her dress and running over everything in her head.

Her thoughts were clearing, she realized. She no longer felt as fuzzy as she had those first few days, or as confused. She still tired quickly, but the aches and pains caused by the accident had lessened, and she no longer had to take painkillers all the time.

She closed her eyes. Her memories of the past eight years were still missing. And yet... as the trees around the deck moved, she felt the dappled light on her face, and saw images flickering at the corner of her vision similar to the movement of the leaves. Would they ever become clearer? Or would they always remain this vague and indistinct?

It didn't matter, she decided. The doctor had told her it could take weeks, months, or years for her memory to come back, if it came back at all. It had only been nine days since she'd whacked her head on the pavement. She wasn't going to stress about it.

Finishing off her drink, she went back into the living room, sat at the desk, and pulled her notepad to her. At some point, she'd printed out a last-minute wedding list off the internet. Time to double check everything and follow up on some of the smaller bits and pieces. Then she'd start ringing her friends and family to tell them it was still on.

She called the local beauty salon to check the time that she was due to have her nails done the day before. Then phoned her hairdresser and asked if she could pop in the next day to discuss an alternative style to cover the wound on the back of her head. Each call took a long time as Noelle had told them all about the accident, and she had to explain each time what had happened, and how she was feeling.

Next, she called her local travel agent to double check on the arrangements for their honeymoon in Fiji. She studied the card while the phone rang, and then when the receptionist answered, asked to speak to Jill.

"Hi Jill," she said when put through to her. "My name is Phoebe Goldsmith. I'm calling to confirm that everything's okay for my honeymoon in Fiji next week." She tried not to giggle as she said it. She was getting married!

"Oh!" Jill exclaimed, and then there was a long moment of silence.

"Hello?" Phoebe said.

"Phoebe! Oh, I'm so pleased to hear you're okay. Your mother rang and told me about the accident, and I couldn't believe it."

"Yes, it's been a trying week," Phoebe said for the umpteenth time that morning.

"I… um… I'm a bit confused, though," Jill replied. "Is the wedding going ahead, then?"

"It is," Phoebe said cheerfully. "I know Mum probably said it might not, but I'm feeling much better and have decided not to cancel."

"I'm sorry," Jill said, "I'm a bit confused. After we got the message that the wedding was off, everything was cancelled."

Phoebe's heart skipped a beat. "What? Oh my God, you must have misheard. My mother wouldn't have cancelled anything without checking with me."

"I don't think it was your mother," Jill said.

Now Phoebe was confused. "But you said you spoke to Mum—"

"That was just a few days ago," Jill said. "I'm talking about last Thursday."

Phoebe frowned. "What do you mean?"

"Last Thursday, the second," Jill clarified. "I was off sick with flu. I left the temp who covered for me a list of things to do, which included ringing to confirm whether you wanted to book a connection from Fiji airport to the resort. When I came in the next day, she'd left a message on my desk. I've got it here. It says, 'Masters wedding is off, I've cancelled the flights and the Fiji resort as per instructions.'"

Phoebe could barely breathe. "Who did the temp talk to?"

"It doesn't say. I must admit, I was puzzled. I did try to call you, but you didn't answer. Of course now I understand why. When your mother rang, she explained that you'd had an accident and that everything was on hold. I was so shocked, it was only when I hung up that I thought it was a bit strange when we'd already been informed the wedding was cancelled. But she'd asked me not to ring you because you needed rest, so I just assumed I was the one who was confused, which is normally the case."

Phoebe sat very still in her chair. "So let me get this straight. The temp called someone last Thursday to check on some details, only to be informed that the wedding was off?"

"That's right."

Last Thursday—the day of her accident. "Do you know what time?"

"Um… late-ish, I think. Yes, the note says seven p.m. We open late on Thursdays, but it was quiet, and she was catching up on calls."

Phoebe knew she'd had the accident around seven-fifteen. The police had turned up to tell Rafe around eight p.m.

"Did I make a mistake?" Jill asked, concerned.

"No, it's fine. Thank you. Have a nice day." Phoebe hung up.

For a long time, she just sat there in a daze. Only that morning, she'd thought that her brain was back to normal, but suddenly it refused to function, and she couldn't bring herself to process what she'd just been told.

It was all a big misunderstanding, surely. Someone had gotten the wrong end of the stick, misinterpreted something that someone else had said. There was a simple explanation for all of this, and no need to panic.

Deep down, though, she knew that wasn't the case.

Something had happened that evening. Her gut instinct had been right all along.

Feeling a bit dizzy, she got up and walked through the living room and into the bedroom. Not sure why she'd done so, she sat on the bed.

She was so tired. She should have a sleep for a while. But she felt sick—she couldn't possibly sleep.

It was then that her gaze fell on the door. She'd closed it behind her as she'd gone in. On the back was a cinema poster of *La La Land*, stuck with Blu-Tac, and a corner of it had loosened and peeled away.

Rising, she went over to it and took the poster down. Behind it, the door had a huge hole. Someone had hit it hard, with a heavy object, or maybe a fist.

Phoebe stared at it for a long while. Then she went back to the bed and lowered herself down.

Suddenly, the house felt full of secrets. They'd all been keeping something from her—Rafe, her sisters, her mother. Who had the temp spoken to on the night? It must have been Rafe. He'd told them the wedding was cancelled because he was angry at something she'd done on the Thursday night. He hadn't wanted to marry her after all.

But it didn't make sense, because he'd been so loving over the past week, so keen to keep the wedding on.

Was it her mother? Had Noelle taken it upon herself to cancel their wedding because she was worried about something she'd seen? Or Bianca? Was that why her sister had seemed upset?

There was no way of knowing, and nobody would tell her the truth. She couldn't trust anyone, least of all herself.

Her head was throbbing now, pounding at the base of her skull. Like a zombie, she went into the kitchen and took some painkillers, then returned to bed. She lay down and curled up around the pillow.

Even though the wind was starting to howl, she could barely keep her eyes open, and she faded into sleep gratefully, finding relief in oblivion.

Chapter Twenty-Two

Rafe pulled up outside the house and got out of the car. The wind whipped around him, almost knocking him over, and he cast a look up at the sky, pursing his lips at the sight of the tall trees almost bowed over. It wasn't the first time the Northland had been subjected to a cyclone, and, the previous June, one had devastated the Bay of Islands, destroying houses and shops alike. Hopefully this one wouldn't be as bad, as it wasn't raining as severely as before, but no doubt there would be a lot of damage in the area.

He bent back down and reached across to the passenger side, retrieving the large bouquet of red roses he'd bought on the way home. Shielding them with his jacket from the wind, he locked the car and headed for the front door.

On the whole, despite the bad weather, it had not been a bad day. His team had attended a call out at a large accident on state highway one, and they'd dealt with it efficiently, earning themselves a pat on the back from the station officer. The night shift would have a tough time as there were trees going down all over the place and there would be flooding before the night was out, but he was done for the day. He was tired, but he had a spring in his step as he headed up the path. Things were going well with Phoebe, and last night she'd said she was going to marry him. It was more than he'd hoped for so soon after her accident, and for the first time he felt that maybe, just maybe, things were going to be all right.

He opened the door, walked in, and stopped. It was nearly six thirty and therefore still a couple of hours until sunset, but the weather had cast an odd orange light over the Northland. The house was dark and something felt... off. He closed the door behind him and walked in, dropping his keys on the table. "Phoebe?"

"In here," she called.

He turned toward her voice and walked into the bedroom.

She hadn't turned on any lights in there either. She was sitting on the bed, her back against the pillows, watching the trees whipping about, although she looked up at him as he came in. She glanced at the flowers in his hand, but she didn't smile.

"What's up?" He placed the bouquet on the chair and walked around to her side. "Are you feeling ill?"

She didn't say anything. Seeing a crumpled piece of paper in her hand, he bent, took it, and unraveled it. It was a poster of *La La Land*.

Slowly, he looked at the door. He stared at it for a moment, then turned back to her.

"I spoke to the travel agent today," she said. "I rang to make sure the arrangements were all okay for the honeymoon."

He sat on the edge of the bed, not sure where this was going.

"She told me that a member of the agency had spoken to someone the night of my accident. They'd rung to check on something, and the person they spoke to told them the wedding was off, and to cancel the holiday."

For a moment, Rafe couldn't breathe, his throat tightening with panic.

"Was it you?" she said softly.

He shook his head.

For the first time, she showed some emotion, a touch of fury lighting her eyes. "Don't lie to me, Rafe."

"I'm not lying."

"You haven't stopped since the day I woke up in hospital. I've had this feeling deep in the pit of my stomach that something wasn't right, and I've kept asking everyone, but nobody will tell me the truth. Is it some big conspiracy? Are you all in on it together?"

He looked at his hands, his heart sinking. He'd known this moment was going to come, but, like a coward, he'd kept putting it off.

"Talk to me," she snapped. "What is it? Did you have an affair or something?"

He lifted his head, alarmed. "No, of course not."

"What, then? What could possibly have happened for you to cancel our honeymoon that Thursday?"

"It wasn't me, Phoebe. It must have been you."

She stared at him. "Why would I do that?"

He hesitated, knowing that telling her the truth meant losing her.

She swung her legs around and got up.

"Where are you going?" he asked, standing too.

"I'm leaving. I'm done with being lied to. I obviously can't trust a single word you've said."

"Don't go." He moved in front of the door, blocking her exit.

"Get out of my way." Her eyes glittered dangerously.

He shook his head, and a dull resignation settled over him like a fine mist. He was going to lose her anyway if he didn't tell her. "I'll tell you everything," he said. "I swear. Just don't go."

She stood there, chest heaving with emotion, glaring at him. "How do I know it's the truth though?"

"Sweetheart, I haven't lied to you. There are just some things I haven't told you."

She gave a short, humorless laugh and walked away then, across the room. "You think I'm going to be impressed by semantics?" She turned and glared at him again. "You're supposed to be my fiancé. The one person I can trust more than anyone else in the world. Do you know how I feel right now? I feel fucking violated."

He swallowed hard. "I know. And I'm so sorry. I thought I was doing the right thing."

She didn't reply. He walked forward and stopped a few feet from her. Outside, one of the chairs on the deck skittered across the wood, blown by the wind. He should go out, stack them all, and tie them down, but nothing could have made him leave at that moment. They stood in front of the sliding doors, cast in the odd, deep-orange light, the sun slowly dying, like their relationship.

No, it wasn't going to end. He refused to think that. He'd told her after the accident that he was going to make this work. He still was.

Somehow.

"We had an argument that Thursday," he said, shoving his hands in the pockets of his jeans so he wasn't tempted to reach out to her. "I got home from work around six-fifteen, and you were working out in the spare room. You told me you'd been there over an hour. I was worried about the amount of time you were spending on fitness—we've argued about it a lot. I said that you should have a shower and have dinner with me. You told me you were going out for a run first. I'd had a tough day at work, I was tired, and I lost my temper. I said that I was fed up with being second place to your fitness program. You said if I felt like that, it was my fault, and you weren't going to change the way you were."

He swallowed hard at the memory. "It blew up into a huge argument, the worst we've ever had. Eventually, you put your running shoes on and just left. I was frustrated and angry, and I punched the door." He indicated the hole in the wood. "I guess the travel agent rang you as you headed out, and you were cross and frustrated, and said the wedding was off. The next thing I knew was an hour later when the police were knocking on my door to tell me you'd had an accident."

Phoebe was frowning, clearly trying to process the information. "It explains some things," she said eventually, "but not everything. Was the whole argument about me working out? Why were you so angry about it? It doesn't make sense."

"It wasn't just the working out." Rafe suddenly felt exhausted, and he sank onto the edge of the bed. "We'd been having… issues, the past few months."

She folded her arms. "What kind of issues?"

"About the move to Auckland."

"I knew it," she said. "After all the time I'd spent building up the bridal shop, I couldn't understand why I was so happy to go. I obviously wanted to back you up with your promotion, but it was always going to cause problems between us. You knew how I felt about the shop. How much I'd put into it. Why did you think I could give it up just like that?"

"Phoebe," he said quietly, "I was the one who didn't want to go."

She studied him, blinking. "What?"

"You went for the job at Mackenzie's without telling me. Six weeks ago, you came home and told me you'd been for an interview and they'd offered you the job. I thought you'd gone to the city for shopping; I didn't know anything about the interview. You said you really wanted to take it, and asked me to apply for a transfer to the Auckland Fire Station."

Her lips parted. "But…"

"I'm happy here," he said, somewhat resentfully, angry that they were having the same argument all over again. "We've got a lovely house, a good social life, great friends, and you have your family. I love my job here. I don't want promotion. I'd be content with getting married and just being together. I wanted to start a family right away— it was your choice to wait. But although I was angry in the beginning, I said I'd go with you because I love you, and I want you to be happy."

Her face filled with frustration. "I don't understand. Why would I want to leave the bridal shop? Why did I throw myself into running marathons, for fuck's sake? It's not me. What the hell happened to change me that much?"

"It was your father," Rafe said simply, trying not to think about the promise he'd made to Noelle. She'd understand that it had to come out eventually, surely.

"Yes, my father died," she snapped, "I get it. I know how upset I would have been. But I'm a realist; I know that shit happens. I don't believe that single event would have turned my life upside down so completely."

"It wasn't what happened, it was how it happened." Rafe wished he could save her from this, but it was too far gone now. The cyclone was almost on them, and all he could do was hang on tightly and do his best to repair the damage when it was done. "That day, you were due to meet your father for lunch. You were going to talk to him about the wedding preparations, because I'd asked him for your hand just a week before. You texted him at twelve thirty and said you'd pick him up at one o'clock, and he texted back that he was looking forward to it. Noelle was at work. But on the way out from the shop, you met a friend you hadn't seen for a while and got chatting. You texted your dad again and said you were going to be thirty minutes late. You turned up at the house at one-thirty, and found him on the floor. He was already dead."

Phoebe's hand rose to cover her mouth.

"The thing is, you'd had that text from him just after twelve-thirty. And you convinced yourself that if only you'd turned up at one, as you'd promised, you'd have been in time to help him."

Slowly, she lowered herself onto the edge of the bed.

"It changed you," Rafe said. "You couldn't cope with that knowledge. You sunk into a deep depression for about four months. It was awful. I couldn't reach you. Eventually, I begged you to get help, and you ended up seeing a grief therapist. They suggested that exercise is a good way to get the endorphins going, and so you started running in the morning."

He sighed. "But you... I don't know... became addicted to it, I guess. It was something you could focus on. In the beginning I didn't say anything; I was just relieved that you were feeling better. We moved in together, and things were going okay. But the more you ran, the more you wanted to run. You did the Kerikeri half marathon and loved it. You ran to raise money for the Heart Foundation, and that became incredibly important to you. It was as if you thought you could counterbalance the guilt of what you'd done by helping others who had heart problems. It became an obsession. You turned vegetarian, and exercised all the time. It overtook everything. I... I felt as if I was losing you."

He stopped and swallowed. Something banged against the window, a bird or a branch from the tree, making them both jump, but neither of them turned to look.

"I just wanted you to be happy," he said softly. "But I wasn't enough for you. The bridal shop was no longer enough, either. You got impatient with sewing one gown after another—you wanted something bigger, better. You just became so... intense, and you couldn't understand why everyone else seemed content with their small lives. You were quite harsh with Bianca, and told her that she had no ambition, and that—"

"Stop it!" Phoebe put her face in her hands. "I can't bear it. Don't tell me any more."

Chapter Twenty-Three

A vast whirlwind of emotions overwhelmed Phoebe, so strong it made her head spin.

"Hey." Rafe moved closer to her and pulled her into his arms. "Come on, I'm sorry."

But she stood again, dashing away tears. "Why didn't you tell me all this?"

"Your mum asked me to wait. Don't blame her—she was worried about the effect it would have on you. She just wants you to get better."

So, they *had* all been in on the deception. "You're my fiancé," Phoebe said desperately. "You should have known me better than that. It's not my mother's place to tell you what to do. Why weren't you honest with me? Why didn't you tell me about our argument?"

Rafe stood too. He looked distraught, his eyes filled with pain. "You seemed so different without all those memories dragging you down. It was as if a huge weight had been lifted. I knew that if I told you, you'd say you didn't want to leave, because you didn't have that overwhelming guilt and grief driving you forward. And it would have been so easy for me to say 'All right, sweetheart, let's stay.' How could I not? It's what I want in my heart. But I knew that when you got your memory back, you'd hate me for it. You'd see it as a betrayal, because I know what was important to pre-accident Phoebe. I couldn't push my own agenda, that wouldn't have been fair."

She gave a short, incredulous laugh. "You were being *altruistic?*"

"I'm not saying that. I know it was cowardly. You don't have to tell me that."

Phoebe didn't know what to think. He hadn't told her because he'd been trying to protect her. She'd accused him of having an affair with Bianca, and had said several times that she didn't understand why they were leaving, implying it was his fault, but he hadn't leapt to his own defense.

She was incredibly angry with both him and her mother—and, presumably, the rest of the family, because they must all have been in on it—and yet she wasn't stupid. They all loved her, and they'd done what they thought was best for her. She'd obviously suffered last year, and they'd all been worried about her. And she had a brain injury. Her mother must have been out of her mind with fear that being told what had happened with her father would have sparked it all off again.

She turned away and walked up to the window, looking out at the wild night.

She was full of emotion, and yet, she also felt oddly distant too. It was as if they'd been to see a movie, watching the drama being played out amongst a group of characters that she had no connection with once she'd left the movie theater. Everything that had happened last year remained a mystery to her. She could understand why she'd reacted that way when her father had died, but right now she felt puzzled by the depth of her guilt. It wasn't her fault that her father had died. Sure, it was possible that she might have been able to save him if she'd turned up at one o'clock, but equally maybe he'd died at 12:45, and she would still have been too late. Or maybe, even if she'd been there, she wouldn't have been able to save him.

Although she didn't practice any religion, she'd been brought up a Christian, and she had faith that there was something beyond the world that she could see and hear. She believed that everything happened for a reason, and she had a basic hope that people were generally good and honest at heart. Maybe that was naive, and she'd become so cynical over the last eight years that her father's death had taken a much bigger toll than it might have done when she was eighteen. But the truth was that Old Phoebe had gone, and might never come back.

Rafe moved to stand behind her, although he didn't touch her. "Are you okay?" he said softly.

"My head hurts," she whispered.

"Do you want me to get you some painkillers?"

She nodded, and he walked off. She heard him moving about in the kitchen, and then he came back in with a glass of water and a couple of pills. She took them from him and swallowed them, washing them down with a few mouthfuls of water. Taking the glass from her, he put it on the bedside table, then came back to her.

"I'm sorry," he said.

She watched a dead palm leaf lift in the wind, flipping over and over before a gust tossed it down the bank into the river. "It's so powerful—it makes me feel so helpless."

"Are you talking about the weather or the situation?"

She gave him a wry glance. "Both." She turned to face him, leaning against the window, resting her head on the glass. He did the same, his hands deep in his pockets. He was so handsome, it made her heart ache.

"I'm sorry," he said again. "For not telling you everything."

She just shook her head. "Do you think my memory will ever come back?"

"I don't know."

"What if it doesn't?"

"What do you mean?"

She shrugged. "Should I carry on the way I was, even though I don't associate with that girl anymore, just in case she suddenly returns? Or do I accept that she's gone, and just be the person I am now?"

He didn't say anything, just looked down at his feet.

"You prefer me the way I am now," she said softly.

He lifted his gaze back to hers. "I love you no matter which Phoebe you are."

It was sweet, but she knew he was lying. He'd told her that he didn't want to move to Auckland. He'd said she'd become intense, and that he felt as if he was losing her. He'd liked the fact that she'd lost the hollows in her cheeks, and was putting on a little weight. He loved her, and he would have loved her no matter how she'd changed, but equally he'd missed the carefree Phoebe he'd fallen in love with.

"I don't want to remember," she said. Tears welled in her eyes. "I don't want to get those memories back. I don't want to be old Phoebe again." The tears tumbled over her lashes, and she covered her mouth with a hand.

"Aw, hey." He moved closer to her and wrapped his arms around her. "It's okay. Everything's going to be okay."

"I'm sorry." She sobbed into his T-shirt.

"You've got nothing to be sorry about. You've had a really tough time, and you've coped with it the best way you could." He kissed her hair.

"I don't want to move to Auckland," she whispered between sobs. "I don't want to leave the shop."

"It's okay, you don't have to make your mind up now."

"I don't want to run anymore."

He inhaled shakily. "It's all right. You don't have to."

"I don't want to let old Phoebe down, but I don't want to be her anymore."

"Shhh. Come on, you'll make your head worse." Bending at the knees, he picked her up and carried her over to the bed. He climbed on the mattress and leaned against the pillows, Phoebe still on his lap, leaned back, and held her tightly.

She curled up against him, trying not to bawl her eyes out. God, she was so tired. All the emotion had worn her out.

"I'm sorry we argued on Thursday," she whispered. "I'm sorry I made you feel as if you were in second place."

"It doesn't matter now."

"I love you."

"I love you too. Shhh."

She bit her lip hard and closed her eyes.

In less than a minute, she'd fallen into an exhausted sleep.

*

When she awoke, it was dark. She was lying on her side on the bed, Rafe close behind her, her back to his chest. She lifted her head to see that the cyclone was at its height, the house creaking and groaning, the trees bent double in the wind. Rain lashed at the windows, and the sky was devoid of light. She could barely see anything in the room—even the digital clock was black, which meant there had been a power cut.

"Are you okay?" Rafe's voice came out of the darkness.

"I'm thirsty," she said.

"I'll get you a drink." He sat up.

"I guess there's no power," she said. "I'd have loved a cup of tea."

"The camping stove's in the cupboard. I'll boil up some water."

Before she could tell him not to take the trouble, he'd left the room.

She lay there for a moment, testing the back of her head with her fingers, and eventually ripping off the dressing impatiently. The wound was tender but clean, and she could feel the hairs growing back.

Rising, she padded out into the living room and through it to the kitchen. The blue light from the camping stove lit the room, and Rafe was leaning against the counter, waiting for the small saucepan of water to come to the boil.

"Hey," he said. "You should have stayed in bed."

"I wanted to get up." She felt surprisingly awake. "Wow, that storm's something."

"Isn't it?"

"I hope all the ducks are safe," she said.

"I'm sure they're tucked well away under the pier."

"It's scary being so out of control."

He looked at her, maybe not sure whether she was talking about the weather again. "How's your head?"

"It's all right. I want to stop taking the painkillers. They make me feel fuzzy."

"Okay."

She looked into the pot, seeing little bubbles forming on the base of the pan. "It's nearly there."

He took two mugs, put a teabag in them, and as the water started to boil, poured it over. After waiting a minute, he removed the bag, added a splash of milk, and handed her a mug.

Sipping it, she walked into the living room and up to the window. Rafe joined her, and they watched the storm for a while. Eventually, he looked down at her. She could barely see him in the darkness, but his eyes glistened.

"What?" she asked.

"I can't believe you're still here," he said, his voice husky. "I was convinced that once I told you everything, you'd walk out."

"Old Phoebe might have done. New Phoebe's a bit more practical." She could just see his lips curve up a little. "It's too easy to make big dramatic gestures," she said. "To flounce around and cast blame and walk out. Look where that got me last time. We're grownups, aren't we? It makes more sense to work through stuff, to talk about it."

He nodded.

"You should have told me," she said. "Everything, at the beginning. It wasn't right to keep it from me."

"I know."

"Even if it had made me feel bad, I should have been told. I'll have words with my mother about pressuring you to keep it a secret."

"She only wanted the best for you," he said.

Phoebe smiled at that. Even though it had gone against his wishes, he'd done what her mother asked, and he refused to blame her for it. She lifted a hand and stroked his cheek. "You really are very sweet."

He turned his head and kissed her palm. "I'm ashamed of that last argument. I hated myself for it, and when the police came, and I thought for a while that I wasn't going to have the chance to apologize for it… It nearly broke me. So, I want to say now that I am sorry for it."

"I know. It's done, Rafe, all water under the bridge."

He cleared his throat and rubbed his nose.

"I meant what I said," she continued. "I don't want to go to Auckland."

His eyes glittered in the small amount of light. "You don't have to make that decision now."

"I do. Because even if I get my memories back, Old Phoebe has New Phoebe to contend with. I think we should start again. I think… I still want to get married on Tuesday."

Rafe inhaled audibly. "You mean that?"

"I do. I'm not about to throw away a lifetime with you because of what's happened. We've both made mistakes and said things we don't mean, I'm sure. I'll understand if you say now that you'd rather wait and see if Old Phoebe comes back, because even if I promise to try to control her, I know it's impossible to say it'll work, but if—"

He put down his tea, took her face in his hands, and kissed her.

Phoebe's lips curved under his, and she closed her eyes and gave herself over to the kiss.

When he finally moved back, she lowered the mug to the table next to his and returned to his embrace. "And Rafe… on Monday, I want to go to the doctor's and have the IUD removed. I want to start trying for a family."

"Oh Jesus." He put his arms around her and hugged her tightly. She bore it for a while, stroking his back, then moved away gently and looked up at him. His face was wet, and when she brushed away the tears with her thumb, he blew out a breath and looked away.

"Maybe we should start practicing now," she murmured. "To make sure we get it right."

His gaze came back to hers. "I don't know what to say." His voice was husky with emotion.

"Then just kiss me." She lifted her lips to his.

To her relief, he returned the kiss, sighing, molding her body to his. She turned her back to the window and leaned against the glass, and took her time to kiss him, just enjoying the knowledge that they were still together, and it wouldn't be long before this man belonged to her, and was hers for life. She felt no regret that she'd agreed to marry him, just relief that she'd finally gotten to the bottom of the problem. The world hadn't ended; the sky hadn't fallen. Rafe was still here with her.

He lifted his head, his nose brushing hers. "You know I love everything about you," he told her fiercely. "Old Phoebe, New Phoebe... They're all different sides of you, and I love them all the same."

Her throat tightened with emotion. She nodded and caught the bottom of his T-shirt in her hands. He lifted his arms, and she pulled it over his head and dropped it to the floor. Then she undid her shorts and slid them off, and removed her own T-shirt.

"Let's go in the bedroom," he said, but she shook her head.

"Here." She slipped her panties down and removed her bra.

Rafe unbuttoned his jeans. "We should take our time," he scolded. "We don't have to rush things."

"We can have an hour of foreplay next time if you like." She pulled him toward her. His erection jutted through his boxers like an iron bar, making her mouth water. "Now, I just want you in me." She tugged the boxers down his legs.

He stepped out of them, sighed as she stroked him, and kissed her again, plunging his tongue into her mouth. Despite her urgings, he stroked her breasts for a while before moving his hand between her legs. His fingers slipped through her folds easily, and he gave a helpless groan, so she knew she was wet and swollen. But he still took time to arouse her, caressing her clit, until she began to gasp and rock against his hand.

Then he put his hands under her butt, lifted her, and pressed her back against the glass.

"You're sure?" he murmured. When she nodded, he lowered her down slowly, impaling her on his erection until he was all the way in.

Tears came into Phoebe's eyes, and he stopped immediately and said, "Oh jeez, did I hurt you?"

She shook her head. "Happy tears," she whispered.

A frown flickered on his brow, but she sank her hands into his hair and kissed him, and he sighed and began to move, holding her tightly as he thrust inside her.

Phoebe kissed him deeply, losing herself in the beauty of being so close to him, so intimate. Behind her, outside, the wind howled, and the trees whipped at the windows, but it only seemed to heighten her emotion, making her feel as if the whole world was taking part in their lovemaking.

She was losing control, and so was Rafe, his thrusts becoming more insistent, his breathing harsh, and she whispered, "Yes, yes," locking her ankles behind his back to encourage him to thrust harder, deeper. So he did, and she leaned back on the glass, letting him have his way, abandoning herself to his strength, his desire, his passion, as he carried them both to the edge, and they tumbled over together.

Tears trickled down her cheeks, and she couldn't stop them, unable to fight the emotion that had been swirling around inside her all day. Even as he swelled and pulsed inside her, Rafe kissed them away, his lips pressing gently over her face. And when he'd done, he withdrew, lifted her off the glass, and carried her through to the bedroom. Placing her on the bed, he curled up behind her and pulled the duvet over them.

"I'm sorry," she said, wiping her face in the dark.

"You've got nothing to apologize for." His voice was husky, and she felt his lips touch her hair.

"I'm happy," she said. "Don't think I'm not."

"I know." His arms tightened around her. "I'm going to be the best husband in the world. I don't ever want to make you cry again."

"I love you."

"I love you, too."

Although the wind continued to whip the trees around, the storm had almost blown itself out. Phoebe lay in the dark, listening to its final sighs, knowing that Rafe was still awake because his hand was tracing patterns on her hip. Safe in his arms, she finally let sleep claim her.

Chapter Twenty-Four

"If you're going to throw up," Elliot said, "just don't do it over my shoes."

"I'm not going to throw up." Rafe spoke with more conviction than he felt.

"You've actually turned green," Elliot stated. "It doesn't go with the outfit at all." The two of them wore dark gray suits, white shirts, and white bow ties.

"Will you leave him alone?" Dominic scolded. Although he was acting as the celebrant at the wedding, he wasn't there in a religious capacity, so he, too, wore a suit rather than his usual vestments. "Or I'll start asking when *you're* getting down on one knee."

Elliot pursed his lips, and Rafe chuckled. Everyone knew that Karen was eager to get hitched. For some reason, though, Elliot was dragging his heels. Rafe was certain his best man wasn't as in love with Karen as she was with him. For a long while, he'd suspected that Elliot's true affections lay elsewhere.

"Now, now," he said to the two guys. "Play nicely on my big day."

He was distracted from their reaction by the sight of Angus McGregor walking purposefully toward them down the aisle between the two rows of white fold-up chairs. His heart began to bang on his ribs as he looked at Angus's serious face. Oh no. Please no…

But as he reached the guys, Angus broke into a smile, and he reached out and clapped a hand on Rafe's arm. "She's here."

Rafe wanted to punch his friend for giving him that moment of hesitation, but it was too beautiful a day, and instead he blew out a long breath and gave a wry smile as they all laughed.

It was dumb to have worried, but what groom doesn't fear the bride not turning up on the day? Knowing that it was all going ahead settled his stomach, and while he waited for Phoebe to arrive, he took a few steps away from the others, toward the fence that ran around the garden.

They'd chosen a boutique hotel in Paihia for their wedding, loving the quaint rooms, the large lawn, the beautiful borders of carefully tended flowers, and, only a few hundred feet away, the beach and the Pacific Ocean that sparkled in the afternoon sun. They'd discussed getting married on the sand, but had decided to use the garden for the ceremony, then have photos taken on the beach, and Kole Graham, their photographer, had promised some amazing shots with the ocean behind them.

Only ten days ago, when Phoebe had first opened her eyes and said, *I'm sorry, I don't know who you are*, Rafe had feared that this day would never come to pass. But he'd been determined to win her back, and now he was being rewarded in the best way possible.

He closed his eyes, half wanting to hold onto this moment forever, the seagulls crying overhead, the smell of the salty sea and the jasmine from the borders in his nostrils, and the excited anticipation of seeing Phoebe sending tingles through him. He felt like a six-year-old who couldn't sleep on Christmas Eve because he suspected Santa was downstairs delivering a train set.

The last few days leading up to their wedding had passed in a blur. He'd been on night shift on Saturday and Sunday, but he'd spent the mornings going over wedding details with his future bride, ringing around to make sure all their friends and family were still coming, and ensuring that everything else was organized.

Rafe had called Jill at the travel agents and had explained everything. Jill had been very understanding, and had said that it was just an unfortunate confluence of events, because if she'd been in the office on that Thursday, she wouldn't have cancelled the holiday for another day or two, because it occasionally happened that stress got to couples who would argue and cancel and then make up.

She'd managed to secure them last-minute flights to Fiji, and she'd then rung the resort they'd originally booked at. The resort had replied that although the lagoon villa they'd originally wanted had now been booked, the honeymoon suite was available, and they were going to upgrade them because of their unfortunate circumstances, so they were now super excited about leaving for their holiday the next day.

He couldn't believe things had ended as well as they had. He really was going to marry the girl of his dreams.

His father and stepmother were there, and his brothers. Was his mum here, too, watching over him? He hoped so, and that she was happy with his choice of bride. He liked to think they would have gotten on well together. Maybe if his and Phoebe's first child was a girl, they might think about calling her Mae, after his mum. The thought made him smile.

"Rafe." Elliot nudged him.

He turned and walked back to the spot in front of the podium, then finally his gaze fell on the archway over the path from the hotel. Phoebe stood there holding Angus's arm, lit by the rays of the afternoon sun, which bounced off the beads on her dress and covered her in sparkles like fairy dust.

Rafe caught his breath. To his shock, his eyes filled with tears.

"Aw," Elliot said.

Dominic patted Rafe on the back. "Top marks for determination," he murmured. "You deserve your prize."

Rafe fought to stop the tears spilling as she walked down the aisle, and thought he'd been successful. But when she stopped next to him, she reached up and brushed her thumb across his cheek, so he knew one must have escaped.

"I knew I'd make you blub," she said cheerfully, although her own eyes were shining. She wore a garland of flowers on her blonde hair, and he couldn't believe that she and Bianca had made the gown—it was like something royalty would wear.

"You look amazing," he whispered. "Like a princess." He swallowed hard. "Still want to marry me, then?"

Her light green eyes were clear, with no sign of anything but honesty. "With all my heart," she said, and they turned to face Dominic, who raised his voice to welcome everyone to the bay.

*

Much later, when the sun was setting, and the hotel staff had lit lanterns around the garden, Phoebe and Bianca walked onto the beach, kicked off their shoes, and let the warm sand trickle between their toes. Although Phoebe had chosen a small wedding, Bianca, Roberta, Libby, and Dominic's daughter Emily had all been her bridesmaids, and they all wore similar gowns, in a champagne color with shoestring straps and floaty skirts. Phoebe thought that Dominic was going to have trouble getting his daughter to take the dress off at the end of the day.

"I'm tempted to get undressed and go for a swim," Phoebe said. "But it would be a shame to waste the underwear before Rafe gets a look at it."

Bianca chuckled. "You'll just have to be careful that you don't take his eye out when you undo the corset."

Phoebe gave a wry smile. She'd put on a little weight over the past ten days, and as a result the dress was… snug. Luckily, the pretty underwear she'd chosen had some boning which held everything in, but she could see her sister's point.

"You look so happy," Bianca said. "I'm glad everything worked out."

"Me too." The look of wonder when Rafe had turned around and seen her in the garden would stay with her forever. "Now we just need to find you your Mr. Right."

Bianca shrugged. "I don't know if I'll ever get married. I'd be quite happy being the old spinster who sews wedding dresses. I'll end up looking like Miss Havisham."

They both laughed. "Is there no one you've got your eye on?" Phoebe asked.

Bianca shook her head. "There have been a couple of guys over the years, but nobody serious."

"I always thought you'd end up with Freddie Brooks," Phoebe said. Freddie had gone to school with them, and Bianca had always had a thing about him, right through their school years. "Did you ever tell him how you felt about him?"

"Yes, around the time we started university. He said he liked me, but he was too young to settle down, and he wanted to see the world. He went into the army."

"Shit, really?"

"Yeah. I saw his mum not long ago—he's a captain now, based somewhere in the Middle East."

"Jeez."

"She's pretty worried about him."

"Does he have a girl here?"

"No idea."

"You could write to him."

Bianca waved a hand. "It's all in the past. He wouldn't want to hear from me."

Reaching out, Phoebe took her sister's hand as they walked along the sand. "I'm so sorry for everything," she said.

Bianca swallowed hard. They'd all been emotional today, and tears hadn't been far from the surface at any point. "Forget about it. I'm just glad you're staying—if it's what you want."

"It is."

Bianca walked quietly for a while. Then she said, "What do you think you'll do if your memory does come back?"

Phoebe bent to pick up a shell. Turning it over in her fingers, she said, "Can you keep a secret?"

"Of course."

"I am remembering things."

Bianca's jaw dropped. "Oh my God."

"Not everything," Phoebe said. "Little flashes, images, from events all over the place.'

"When did this start?"

"The day after the storm. But I haven't told anyone else, so don't tell Rafe. I might tell him while we're away, but I don't want to worry him today."

Bianca surveyed her. "You remember Dad dying?"

"Yes. Bits and pieces of the day."

"How do you feel about it?"

She looked out to sea, at the fishing boats returning to the pier, full of the day's catch, and the way the sun had filled the sea with a deep orange-red, reminding her of the night of the cyclone. "Actually, I'm all right. I can remember some of the angst I felt after Dad died, and how knotted up I was with grief and guilt. But it's tempered by everything I've experienced this week. I think that before, it was so gradual a thing that I didn't notice it building. It was like a cancer, eating away at my soul, and I couldn't stop it. I didn't realize what an effect it was having on everyone around me, especially you and Rafe. I'm ashamed of that."

"You only did what you thought was right," Bianca said. "And we only have one life, probably, so you have to go for your dreams."

"Yes, true. But there's more to life than satisfying your own whims. I don't want to fulfil my every fantasy while treading on my loved ones in the process. I think I'd forgotten how to be content. Losing Dad made me panicky that I was wasting my life and not making the most of every minute. But over the past week, Rafe and I have spent a lot of time… I don't know… just being. And then working with you in the shop—it's been wonderful. I don't want more than that. I don't know why I ever did."

Bianca pulled her to a stop, then threw her arms around her and hugged her.

Phoebe hugged her back. "Born together, friends forever," she whispered fiercely. "Don't let's ever change that."

*

An hour later, Phoebe and her mother sat side by side with their feet propped up on chairs, having a drink while they took a break from dancing. The hotel had opened the large sliding doors leading from the dining room onto their huge deck, and the band had set up there, so dancers could look out at the sea, and in fact some had spilled onto the beach.

"You look so much better," Noelle said. "But you need to be careful you don't wear yourself out."

"Yes, Mum." Phoebe wrinkled her nose.

Noelle looked at the glass in her hand. "Sorry. I must stop doing that. I forget you're all grown up now. It's just hard to switch off being a mum."

"That's okay." Phoebe smiled. "I'd rather you be like that than not care at all."

"I know I've said it before, but I'll say it again," Noelle said. "I'm sorry I didn't tell you about what happened when your father died. And I'm so sorry that Rafe ended up bearing the brunt of it all. He wanted to tell you at the beginning—it was me who asked him not to. I was just so worried it would set you back."

"Don't worry about it." Phoebe held her mother's hand. "It's all behind us now. Everyone did what they thought was best. Now, it's time to think of the future. I wanted to tell you—Rafe and I are hoping to start a family soon."

Noelle pressed her hand to her mouth, her eyes shining. "Oh, sweetheart, that's wonderful news."

"I hoped you'd be happy."

"I'm over the moon. I'm so pleased it all worked out for you."

"The doctor said the injury might affect my ability to conceive, but hopefully there won't be anything wrong."

She'd been wanting to ask her mother something, and she guessed that now was as good a time as any. "What about you? Are there any signs of a man on the horizon?"

Her mother's eyes widened. "Goodness, no. I'm far too old for all that."

"You're fifty-two. You're hardly ancient."

"I loved your dad very much," Noelle said softly. "Nobody could ever replace him."

Phoebe swallowed hard. "I know. But he's been gone over a year. You deserve happiness and companionship too."

"I am happy." Noelle squeezed her hand. "I have the shop, and an active social life. And all my children, and Emily, who'll soon be joined by more grandchildren, hopefully. I don't need a man. Nobody would match up to your dad, anyway."

"I just want you to know that if you did meet someone, it would be fine by me."

"Thank you, darling, but don't you worry yourself about it."

Phoebe opened her mouth to reply, but at that point Roberta turned up with Bianca, both of them flushed and with bright eyes.

"Come on," Roberta said. "It's your wedding day and there's music playing! You need to dance!"

"I have a brain injury," Phoebe protested as her sister pulled her to her feet.

Roberta blew a raspberry. "Angus is over there if you need CPR. Come on!"

Laughing, Phoebe followed her to the other girls dancing in the middle of the lawn. Libby was there, and Elliot's girlfriend Karen, and little Emily, Dominic's daughter, as well as several others.

"You look amazing," Libby said, taking Phoebe's hand, and spinning her around. "That dress is just fantastic. I hope you'll make mine one day."

"Oh, has Mike popped the question?" Roberta asked.

Libby's smile dimmed a little. "No, it was more of a general question."

Phoebe exchanged a glance with her sisters, but refrained from saying anything. None of her family or friends seemed to be in happy relationships. It made her a little sad when she was the happiest woman on earth.

She glanced around the dance floor and spotted Rafe sitting with her brothers, and with Angus, Mike, and some of their other friends. She twirled and blew him a kiss, and he blew one back.

"Aw." Libby bumped shoulders with her.

"He gets you for the rest of your life," Roberta said, pulling her into the center of the circle. "Tonight, you're ours!" And she spun Phoebe around to the music, their laughter joining the sound of the waves on the beach and the smoke from the candles, spiraling off into the night.

*

"They'll all sleep well tonight," Dominic said, smiling at the sight of his sister twirling around, her dress sparkling in the candlelight.

"Sleep wasn't quite what I had in mind," Rafe said.

"Any more of those and you're not going to be good for anything anyway." Elliot gestured to Rafe's whisky glass.

"It's my wedding day. My last day of freedom before the old ball and chain cracks her whip."

Angus snorted. "What a load of shit. I've never seen a man happier to be tied down."

"Anytime she wants to tie me down, she's welcome to," Rafe said.

The rest of them sighed, and Rafe grinned at the thought that he appeared to be the only one who had a girl who set his bed alight.

"That's my sister you're talking about," Elliot said. "I should call you out on a duel."

Rafe stared at him, and then they all started laughing.

"She looks happy," Dominic said, returning their gazes to the girls. They all watched them dancing for a few minutes.

Rafe looked at Elliot to see if he was watching Karen. He wasn't.

Elliot glanced at him, saw his raised eyebrow, and just said, "Don't."

Rafe finished off his drink. He'd nearly screwed up his own relationship; he wasn't about to give advice on everyone else's.

"Uh oh," Dominic said at the sight of Roberta marching toward them.

"Come on." She beckoned her fingers. "There are loads of lovely women out there looking for some attention. You don't really think we'd let you sit here all evening?"

Rafe chuckled. She was so different to her twin sisters. Dark-haired, tall, and slim-hipped, often called Bobcat by her friends and family, she was feisty, sporty, and—Rafe thought privately—somewhat scary. She always wore jeans or shorts and he'd never seen her in a skirt, but tonight she looked amazing in her bridesmaid's dress, and more than one guy at the wedding had their eye on her, he was sure.

She grabbed Angus's hand and pulled him to his feet. "I haven't finished my drink," he complained. "And I don't dance."

"Bullshit. Come on." She practically dragged him onto the dance floor.

Rafe laughed. "Come on," he said to the others, leading them toward the girls. Grabbing his wife by the waist, he swung her to face him. She threw her arms around him, and he hugged her tightly.

"You're mine," she said fiercely in his ear. "Forever and ever."

"Till death do us part," he said, and kissed her.

*

Much, much later, Rafe swept his new bride up into his arms and carried her into their room while the others cheered behind them. The bed was covered with rose petals, and there was a huge teddy bear holding a giant Just Married sign in the middle.

Phoebe laughed as she saw it and waved to her sisters, who waved back before Elliot winked at them and closed the door.

"What a wonderful evening," she said with a sigh.

"And it's not over yet." Rafe carried her to the bed, turned, and fell backward so she landed on top of him.

She squealed, and he rolled so she was pinned beneath him, both of them tangled in the skirt of her gown.

"You smell of whisky," she said, sinking her hands into his hair.

"That's because I've been drinking whisky." He kissed her.

"Mmm." She put both hands on his chest and pushed him back a little. "Are you drunk?"

"Nope. I'm… merry."

She chuckled and smoothed her hands over his shoulders. He'd long ago lost the jacket and the bow tie. His hair was disheveled, and there was a hint of five o'clock shadow on his jaw.

"You look amazing," she said.

He stared at her, and then gave a short laugh. "If I look amazing, there isn't a word in the dictionary to describe you."

"You like the dress?"

"I love the dress. I love what's underneath it even more." He tried to find the bottom of her gown to slide his hand beneath it, and failed.

She giggled at his impatient frown. "Don't worry, you can take it off in a minute. I have a surprise for you underneath."

"Ooh. Way to tempt a new husband." He moved to the side, turning her to face him, kissed her for a while, then lifted his head and kissed her nose. "How are you feeling?"

"I'm fine."

"Not too tired? We have the rest of our lives together, you know."

She shook her head. They'd spent the previous night apart as she'd stayed at her mother's house with her two sisters, and just that one night without him had been almost more than she could bear.

"We're off to Fiji tomorrow," he reminded her. "I'm sure you could do with a good night's sleep."

Pushing up, she rose from the bed and stood in front of it. "You see what's beneath this dress, and then you decide whether you want to sleep." She turned and presented her back to him.

Rafe came to stand behind her, and slowly undid the hidden zip to the base of her spine. With a little sigh, she pushed the dress down, and it fell to the floor in a billow of silk.

She turned to face him, and was able to catch the look of desire on his face as he saw her underwear, complete with the garters and white stockings.

"You look amazing," he whispered, tracing a finger across the lace that covered the top half of her breasts, which were propped up by the stiff corset.

She shivered. "I love you."

His gaze came up to meet hers, and he smiled. "I love you too." His eyes took on a naughty glint. "Can you move in this thing? Because I totally want to do you in it."

Her eyes widened. "Jeez. Mr. Romantic."

"Hey, I'll do you on top of the rose petals. How's that for romance?"

Picking her up, he tossed her onto the bed, where she fell, bouncing on top of the teddy bear and sending rose petals flying. He lifted her dress up and laid it carefully over a chair, then began to undo his shirt buttons.

"Leave your clothes on," she said. "You look like James Bond."

He grinned, toed off his shoes, and climbed onto the bed. Pushing the teddy off, he moved on top of her and lowered himself down.

"Hello, Mrs. Masters," he murmured, kissing her neck.

"Mmm. Hello, husband." She slid her arms around him, then lifted her left hand behind his back. The moonlight glinted off her wedding band.

Rafe lifted his head, looked over his shoulder to see what she was doing, then smiled and brought his left hand across to hold hers. He turned her hand over and kissed the band.

"I'm kissing your ring," he said. His eyes glinted. "Wouldn't be the first time."

"Rafe! Oh my God."

"In fact, I think I might kiss it again tonight." Lifting up, he caught her arm and rolled her onto her front, then kissed down to her butt. She tried to roll back, but he pinned her down, sliding his hand up her stockings to her pretty panties and pulling the elastic out in an attempt to kiss her there.

The air filled with the sounds of their laughter, as the moon rose in the night sky, and a morepork hooted in the nearby pohutukawa tree, its cries mingling with the sounds of the sea.

Newsletter

If you'd like to be informed when my next book is available, you can sign up for my mailing list on my website, http://www.serenitywoodsromance.com

I also send exclusive short stories and sometimes free books!

About the Author

Serenity Woods lives in the sub-tropical Northland of New Zealand with her wonderful husband and gorgeous teenage son. She writes hot and sultry contemporary romances. She would much rather immerse herself in reading or writing romance than do the dusting and ironing, which is why it's not a great idea to pop round if you have any allergies.

Website: http://www.serenitywoodsromance.com
Facebook: http://www.facebook.com/serenitywoodsromance
Twitter: https://twitter.com/Serenity_Woods

Printed in Great Britain
by Amazon